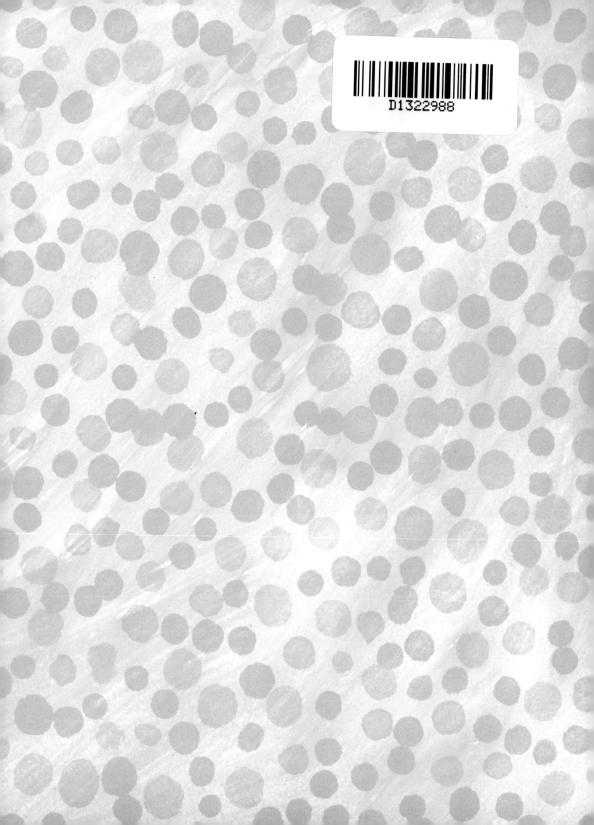

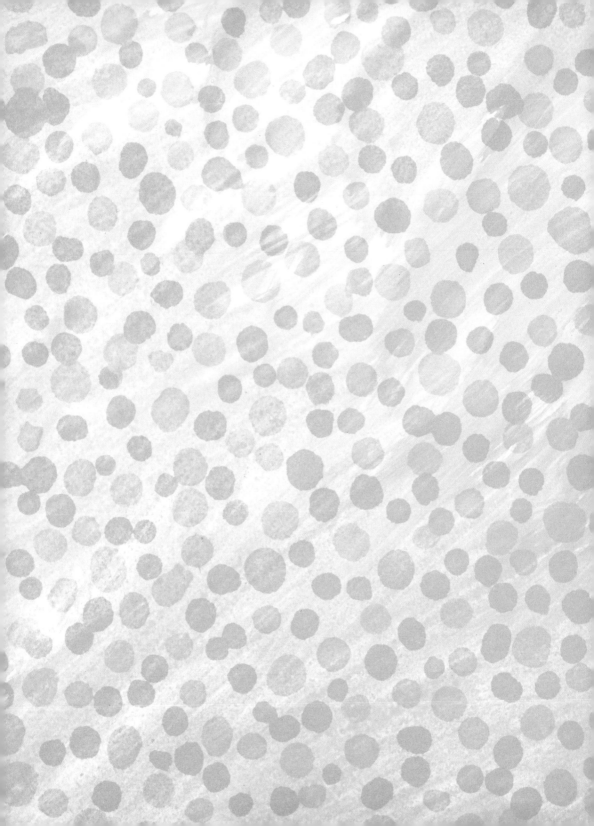

# This book belongs to

~~~~~~~~~~~~~~~~~~~~~~~~~~~~~~~~~~~~~~~~~~~~~~~~~~~~~~~~~~~~~~~~~~~~~~~~~~~~~~~~~~~~~~~~~~~~~~~~~~~~~~~~~~~~~~~~~~~~~~~~~~~~~~~~~~~~~~~~~~~~~~~~~~~~~~~~~~~~~~~~~~~~~~~~~~~~~~~~~~~~~~~~~~~~~~~~~~~~~~~

First published in 2019 by Miles Kelly Publishing Ltd
Harding's Barn, Bardfield End Green, Thaxted, Essex, CM6 3PX, UK

Copyright © Miles Kelly Publishing Ltd 2019

10 9 8 7 6 5 4 3 2 1

Publishing Director Belinda Gallagher
Creative Director Jo Cowan
Editorial Director Rosie Neave
Senior Editors Claire Philip, Amanda Harrison
Designers Jo Cowan, Venita Kidwai, Simon Lee
Image Manager Liberty Newton
Production Elizabeth Collins, Jennifer Brunwin-Jones
Reprographics Stephan Davis, Callum Ratcliffe-Bingham
Assets Lorraine King

ISBN 978-1-78617-861-9

Printed in China

British Library Cataloguing-in-Publication Data
A catalogue record for this book is available from the British Library

## ACKNOWLEDGEMENTS
Cover illustration: Veronica Montoya (Advocate Art)
All other artwork from the Miles Kelly Artwork Bank

Made with paper from a sustainable forest

www.mileskelly.net

# A Story a Day

Compiled by Tig Thomas

## MILES KELLY

# The Hound and the Hare

**O**ne day a hound saw a hare and chased her until he had caught up with her. The hare didn't know what to think. One moment the dog would lunge and snap at her. The next he would leap about, as if he wanted to play.

At last the tormented hare gasped, "I wish you would show your true colours. If you are my friend, why do you bite me? If you are my enemy, why do you play with me?"

The hound paused to consider the question and the hare took her chance to escape. She knew the answer – anyone who plays double is not a true friend.

# The Sunflower

There was once a sea nymph with long golden hair called Clytie. She wore beautiful green gowns woven of seaweed and lived in the very depths of the ocean. One day, she heard a mermaid singing a song about the golden light hanging in the sky, and she longed to see it.

Clytie swam to the water's surface and climbed onto the shore. There she saw the sun for the first time! It was so beautiful that she stood gazing at it all day long.

As night fell she looked down into the water at her reflection. Her golden hair had become yellow petals, her green gown was now made of leaves and her tiny feet had become roots. She had become a sunflower!

And to this very day, all sunflowers turn on their stems so that they can gaze upon the sun as it travels across the sky.

# The Giant who Counted Carrots

High on a mountainside lived a giant who spent his days growing carrots. One day, he came across some young women, dipping their toes in a rock pool.

The giant hid and watched from afar, and he fell in love with one, whose name was Elizabeth. When they skipped away, the giant felt sad. He decided he would try to win the girl's heart. He lined the rock pool with silver, hid again and waited for the girls to return.

When they came back, the girls were astonished to see the pool shining like silver. Elizabeth looked into the pool and heard a voice telling her to step into the water. As soon as she did so, she found herself in the giant's garden.

The giant asked Elizabeth to marry him, but she wanted to go back to her family. The giant hoped she would stay with him and change her mind. As a gift he made her a magic staff. Anything it touched turned into an animal.

One day, the giant showed Elizabeth his carrot fields. Elizabeth asked how many he grew, and while he was busy counting, she touched the staff to a stone. It became a horse, and she leapt on its back and rode away home.

With Elizabeth gone, the giant realized that he had been lonely on his own. So he used his staff to change one of his carrots into a dog. The two became best friends, and went on many adventures together.

# The Moon-cake

A little boy was just about to take a bite of his cake when a bigger boy said, "That cake would be much prettier if it was shaped like the moon. I can do that for you."

The little boy liked the sound of that. "Really?" he asked. He cautiously handed his cake to the big boy, who took an enormous bite! The cake was now shaped like a crescent-moon.

"Hey!" cried the little boy.

The big boy grinned. "Oh well — if you don't want a crescent-moon, I'll make it into a half-moon for you." And he nibbled off the horns of the crescent.

When the little boy saw that, he began to wail.

"Calm down," said the big boy. "Remember, just before the new moon comes, the old moon disappears." And with that he swallowed the rest of the cake and ran off!

# The Lambkin and the Little Fish

Long ago, a cruel woman (who was also a witch) hatched a plan to get rid of her two stepchildren. She whispered a spell and *pfff*! The boy became a fish. The witch dropped him into the castle moat. She whispered a second spell and *pfff*! The girl turned into a lamb. The witch turned her out into the meadow.

The next day, the witch ordered a servant to take the lamb to the market to sell. But as the servant led the lamb past the moat the lamb cried out, "I will always love you, brother." And a fish swimming in the moat cried back, "Sister, your love is returned."

The servant realized that the animals were actually the children bewitched. He took them to a kind woman (who was also a witch) and she undid the spell. The children stayed with her, and she taught them good magic — and they lived very happily together for many years.

# The Farmer and his Dog

One day a farmer was hard at work in his field, mending a gap in one of his fences. He had left his young child asleep in a cradle nearby, thinking that the baby would be safe. But when he returned he found the cradle turned upside down! The bedding was torn, and his dog was covered with blood. The farmer thought the dog had attacked the child, so he furiously chased it away.

But when he turned the cradle over, he found his baby unhurt, and noticed an enormous snake lying dead on the floor — bitten by his faithful dog. The farmer called the dog back, washed its wounds and cared for it kindly for the rest of his life.

# The Snowman

**E**arly one morning, the sun rose over a glorious sight. Everything was covered with snow. A woman, a man and their dog went out into their garden. "Let's build a snowman," said the woman.

When they were finished they went back inside, but the dog stayed outside. The snowman watched them go. "Who are those people?" he asked the dog.

"They are my masters," answered the dog. "They let me sleep by the stove – the most beautiful thing in the world."

"I wish to see the beautiful stove!" said the snowman. He shuffled over to the window and peeped in. He saw a strange object with a long pipe. The glow from the fire reached out to him, and he felt very happy.

"How I long to be next to the stove!"

"Don't be silly," said the dog. "You would disappear."

The sun rose high in the sky and the snowman began to feel hot.

"You should stand in the shade, where it's cooler," barked the dog. But the snowman just shook his head.

Little by little he began to melt away. Soon there was nothing left except a broom lying on the ground – for the young man and woman had built the snowman around it.

"Now I see why he loved the stove so much," said the dog. "That's the broom they use to sweep it out."

# The Fox, the Rooster
# and the Dog

**O**ne night, a fox was prowling about when he saw a rooster perched nearby. The fox quickly thought of a plan, and cried, "Good news!"

"What is it?" asked the rooster.

"King Lion has declared that all the animals should live in peace," declared the fox. "From now on, no beast may hurt another."

"Why, that is good news," said the rooster, "and I see someone with whom we can share it."

"Who is it you see?" said the fox.

"My master's dog is coming to meet us," the rooster said but the fox began to run away.

"Will you not stop and tell the dog the good news also?" called the rooster.

"I would," muttered the fox, "but I fear he may not have heard of King Lion's new law."

# The Fisherman Piping

A fisherman once had a great idea for a new way to catch fish. He thought that if he took his flute to the riverbank and played a jolly tune, the fish might hear the music, and come to the surface and dance. Then the fisherman could catch them easily.

So he began to play one merry song after another, but not a single fish put so much as its nose out of the water. The fisherman gave up, laid down his flute, and went back to his old method of just casting his net into the water.

To his astonishment, when he drew the net in, it was heavy with fish! Then the fisherman took up his flute and played again, and as he played, the fish flipped and flapped in the net.

"Ah, you dance now when I play," he said.

"Yes," replied an old fish, "now that we have no choice."

# The Wolf and the Seven Little Kids

**M**other goat had to go to market. As she was leaving she told her seven little kids, "Do not let anyone into the house until I return."

But the wolf saw her leave, and knocked on the door. "Open up! It's your mother, back from her trip — "

"We won't!" said the little kids. "Mum has a soft voice."

So the wolf ate some honey to soften his voice. Then he put his black paws up to the window and asked to be let in. "No!" said the kids, "Mum has white feet!"

So the wolf covered his feet in flour, and this time the kids let him in. One by one he ate them all up!

When mother goat came home she found only one kid remaining — hidden inside the grandfather clock! He told her what had happened.

Then mother goat went and found the wolf. She kicked him so hard that the other kids flew out of his mouth. The wolf fled, and was never seen again.

# The Rabbit's Bride

There was once a woman who lived with her daughter in a cottage. They had a large vegetable patch where they grew delicious cabbages, but one day a rabbit hopped into their garden and began to eat them.

The daughter ran out shouting, "Shoo!"

To her surprise, the rabbit spoke to her. "My dear," it said, "come and live with me in my underground burrow."

"Certainly not!" said the girl. The rabbit leapt away.

The next day the rabbit was back. Once again the girl ran out shouting, "Shoo!"

"I won't eat your cabbages," said the rabbit, "if you marry me and come and live in my burrow!"

Suddenly, the girl had an idea. "I will," she said. She put on her coat and hat and followed the rabbit. When they reached the burrow, the rabbit said, "Make some food. I'm going to invite my family to the wedding."

When the rabbit had gone, the girl took some straw and tied it with twine to make a figure the same size as herself, and dressed it in her coat and hat. Then she ran home.

After a while the rabbit returned. "Hello," he said. But when the figure didn't answer, he examined it and gasped, "Oh no! I've turned her into straw!"

And he scampered away, promising never to eat cabbages again!

# The Ant and the Dove

**O**nce upon a time, a thirsty ant went to the stream for a drink. However, as he reached down to take a sip, he fell in. He was on the point of drowning when a dove plucked a leaf and let it fall into the stream. The ant used the last of his strength to scramble onto the leaf, then floated safely to the bank, exhausted but alive.

Soon afterwards, a man came along and saw the dove sitting in the tree. Unnoticed by the dove, he set a trap for her. But the tiny ant saw what the man had done.

The ant raced up to the man and bit him as hard as he could. The man cried out, and the noise startled the dove, who flew off, safe and free. 'Kindness brings rewards,' she thought to herself.

# The Boy who Cried Wolf

There was once a shepherd boy who often got lonely and bored out on the hillside. One day he thought of a plan to amuse himself. He rushed towards his village shouting, "Wolf! Wolf!"

The villagers came running to help. When they realized there was no wolf, they went home grumbling.

A few days later the naughty boy tried the same trick and again the villagers came rushing to help. They were very angry to find they had been tricked a second time.

A few days later, a wolf really did come prowling around the sheep. Of course the boy set off crying, "Wolf! Wolf!"

But the villagers thought that the boy was lying again, so nobody came to his aid — and the wolf enjoyed an excellent dinner.

# The Tall Story

**Five blind men** were sitting by a road one morning when they sensed something near them. The first man put out his hand and felt something rough and solid. "It's a wall!" he said.

One

The second man reached out. "No, it's a spear," he said.

Two

The third man felt too. "No, don't be silly, it's a piece of rope."

The fourth man stretched out and wrapped two arms around something, "No, it's definitely a tree trunk."

Three

And the fifth man argued, "You are all wrong, I can feel a snake."

A boy nearby heard their argument. "You're all wrong. It's an ELEPHANT!"

Four

The first man stopped touching the elephant's side, the second man let go of his tusk, the third man dropped the tail, the fourth man stepped away from the leg, and the fifth man took his hands off the trunk. And they never quarrelled again.

Five

# The Little Matchgirl

**It was winter and in the biting cold** a poor little girl was walking barefoot through the streets.

In her ragged old apron she carried bundles of matches. She had been trying to sell them all day, but no one had bought any.

In all the windows of the houses around her, lights were shining – all the families were celebrating New Year's Eve with big roast dinners. When the little girl reached a sheltered corner formed by two houses, she sank down, exhausted. She dared not go home – her father would be angry that she hadn't sold any matches.

The little girl blew on her hands to try to bring them back to life. Then she thought that if she lit a match, it might give her warmth.

She drew one out and struck it firmly against the wall. It gave out a bright flame, like a little candle, and when she held her hands over it, the match was warm and wonderful. It flared up, and when the light fell upon the bricks, it was as if they became transparent and she could see inside the house.

There was a table on which a roast goose steamed away gloriously on a big platter! But then the match went out.

The little matchgirl hurried to light another match. Suddenly, she was sitting under a beautiful Christmas tree.

The girl stretched out her hand to touch it… but the match went out.

'Just one more,' the little matchgirl decided, and in the brightness stood her grandmother.

"Grandmother!" she cried. "Can I stay with you?"

And her grandmother held the girl in her arms, warm and safe from the cold forever and ever.

# The Master of all Masters

**A** **servant girl went to a fair** to find work, and luckily enough an old gentleman hired her. When they were back at his house he told her that he had his own, very particular names for many things and she would have to learn them. Then he asked her what she would call him.

"Why, master or mister, or whatever you please sir," she said.

"You must call me 'master of all masters'," he replied, before pointing to his bed. "And what would you call this?"

"A bed or whatever you please, sir."

"No, that's my 'barnacle'. And what do you call these?" he said pointing to his trousers.

"Breeches or trousers, or whatever you please, sir."

"You must call them 'squibs and crackers'. And what would you call her?" pointing to the cat.

"Cat or kit, or whatever you please, sir."

"You must call her 'white-faced simminy'. And this," pointing to the fire, "what would you call this?"

"Fire or flame, or whatever you please, sir."

"You must call it 'hot stocks'. What would you call this?" he went on, pointing to some water.

"Water or wet, or whatever you please, sir."

"No, 'pondalorum' is its name. And what do you call all this?" asked he, as he pointed to the house.

"House or cottage, or whatever you please, sir."

"You must call it 'high topper mountain'."

That night the girl woke up to find the house full of smoke! She woke up her master, shouting "Master of all masters, get out of your barnacle and put on your squibs and crackers. For white-faced simminy has got a spark of hot stocks on her tail, and unless you get some pondalorum, high topper mountain will be all on hot stocks!" And they escaped unharmed.

# The Cat and the Birds

There once lived a cat who heard that the birds living in a nearby aviary had fallen ill. The cat decided that this would be the ideal opportunity for him to catch them, so he disguised himself as a doctor and set off for the aviary.

Once there, the cat knocked at the door, and asked after the health of the birds.

"We shall be much better," came the reply through the closed door, "when we have seen the last of you!"

# The Six Swans

Many years ago, a king married a witch's daughter. Though she was beautiful, she had a mean heart.

Now, the king already had seven children — six boys and a girl — who he loved dearly. But he didn't tell his new wife about them until after they were married, because he knew she would be terribly jealous.

The queen decided to get rid of the children. She made some enchanted shirts and threw one over each boy, but the girl ran away and hid in the forest.

As soon as the shirts touched their backs the boys became swans and flew away!

The next morning, the girl decided she had to find her brothers and help them. She walked all day, and was just about to settle down to sleep when six swans landed all around her and transformed back into her brothers!

"We must be swans by day," said the eldest brother. "But you can break the spell if you go without speaking for six years and sew six shirts from white flowers."

The girl agreed at once, and the very next morning she began to sew. As she worked, a king came riding by. He fell instantly in love with her and asked her to be his queen. She could not speak, but she nodded. The king took her to live in his castle, and even though she remained silent, the two were happy. Every day she worked on the shirts.

But the king's mother grew suspicious of the silent queen. When the queen gave birth to a baby boy, the king's mother stole the child and blamed its disappearance on the queen! Of course the queen would not speak to defend herself. The king did not know who to believe.

The next morning was the last day of the sixth year. The king watched in amazement as six swans landed on the castle lawn. The queen threw the finished shirts upon the swans' backs and her brothers became human again.

The girl and her brothers hugged each other. Then she turned to the king. "Dear husband, search your mother's rooms — I am sure you will find our baby!"

Sure enough, they found him there safe and sound. The king's mother was asked to leave the kingdom, and everyone else lived together in peace and joy at last.

# Give Me Nothing!

**A** **woodman was carrying** a heavy sack of wood on his back when he tripped over a stone and half of the wood fell out. A passer-by asked, "What will you give me if I replace those pieces of wood?"

"Nothing," said the woodman.

"That's acceptable," agreed the other man. He replaced the wood then asked for his payment. The woodman was baffled.

"I told you I'd give you nothing," he said.

"Yes. And that's what I want. Give me nothing!"

After some quarrel, the two men went to the judge. He listened to both men. He said to the passer-by, "Go and look under the carpet. What do you see there?"

"Nothing." said the man.

"Well, take it and go home," commanded the judge, "That is your payment!"

# How to Choose a Bride

**A** **man wanted to marry** but he didn't know how to choose a bride. He knew of three sisters, all of whom he liked, but he didn't know who would suit him best. He asked his mother's advice, and she said, "See how they eat cheese, then decide." So he invited them all to a meal with him.

When the cheese was served, the eldest cut the rind off so thickly that it included a lot of good cheese. 'She seems wasteful,' thought the man.

The second sister ate her cheese without cutting off any of the rind at all. 'She is not right either,' thought the man. 'She will be careless.'

But the youngest sister cut the rind off cleanly and carefully, and then ate the cheese. The man knew at last, 'She is the right one!'

# The King's New Turban

**O**nce, a man came before a great king and said, "Your Highness, I shall weave you a turban so special that only those who are truly intelligent shall be able to see it."

The king was intrigued by the idea, and said he would like to see such a thing.

After a long while, the man returned. "Here is your priceless turban, great King."

The king tore off the paper and saw… nothing. He didn't want to admit that he wasn't intelligent, so he forced a smile and handed over a great deal of gold to the man. All the nobles who were standing there agreed saying, "How beautiful!"

Then the king summoned his two closest advisors and whispered, "I must be a great fool, for I cannot see the turban!"

They admitted, "O King, nor can we!"

Then they rushed to catch the weaver and have him thrown into prison. But it was too late — the weaver had vanished, along with the gold.

# Why the Bear is Stumpy-tailed

**B**ruin the Bear met Reynard the Fox on a roadside. He was slinking along with a string of fish that he had stolen from a farmer.

"Where did you find those?" asked Bruin.

"Oh, I've been fishing all day and caught them," lied Reynard.

Bruin decided he would learn to fish too. "Oh, it will be easy for you," answered Reynard. "Just go out on the ice, cut a hole and stick your tail down into it. Then hold it there as long as you can. When you can wait no longer, pull your tail out!"

Bruin did as Reynard said, and held his tail down in the hole a long time, until it was entirely frozen. Then he pulled it out – and it snapped off!

And ever since then every bear has had a stumpy tail.

# Hansel and Gretel

Long ago, a woodcutter lived in a forest with his wife and two children, Hansel and Gretel. The family were so poor that there was never enough to eat. The man's wife persuaded him that there were too many mouths to feed, and that he should take the children into the wood and leave them there.

So Hansel and Gretel were left alone in the dark forest. Cold and scared, they walked all night but they could not find their way out.

At last they glimpsed a little house, and when they got close they found it was made of gingerbread! The starving children broke bits off and tucked in. Suddenly the door opened and an old witch came out.

She seized the children and – deciding that Hansel looked tasty but a little thin – locked him in a cage. Poor Gretel was forced to fetch water and cook meals.

One day the witch said, "Your brother must be fat enough to eat by now. Girl, go and see if the oven is hot enough."

Gretel had an idea. "Can you show me how?" she said.

The witch grumbled but bent down close to the oven. Gretel gave her a push and – *clang!* – she shut and bolted the door.

Gretel raced to set Hansel free. They filled their pockets with the witch's treasure and somehow they made their way home. There they found their father alone – their mother had left. Their father was overjoyed to see them, and they lived happily ever after.

# The Tree and the Reed

There was once a huge tree that towered over its neighbours. At its foot grew a small reed. One day the tree said to the reed, "Well, little one, why don't you ever grow taller?"

"I am content with my lot," said the reed. "I may not be grand, but I think I am safe."

"Safe!" scoffed the tree. "I'm too big for anyone to pull up, but they could easily do that to you!"

Soon after this exchange, a storm tore the tree down, causing the tree to regret its boast. But the little reed was able to bend in the wind, and did not break. 'Obscurity brings safety,' thought the reed.

# Foolish Hans

**O**nce upon a time there lived a poor woman and her foolish son, Hans. One day the woman gave Hans a pot of honey, saying, "Sell this, but don't let people talk to you too much." She was afraid that people would bargain with him and he would be outwitted.

Arriving in town, Hans shouted, "Buy my honey!"

The people said, "How much is it?"

Foolish Hans said, "You are talking to me too much!" and he started to walk home.

The flies on the country road swarmed around him. "Buy my honey!" he said. The flies buzzed, so Hans poured his honey on the ground saying, "Now pay me!" The flies ate the honey, but they gave him nothing.

"I am reporting you all to the judge," shouted Hans. "You flies have robbed me!"

Hans went to the court and said, "The flies ate my honey and now they won't pay me."

The judge began to laugh. "Well whenever you see a fly, I suggest you swat it."

Just then a fly landed on the judge's nose, so Hans hit it really hard.

"Ouch! My nose!" cried the judge.

Hans said simply, "You told me to swat flies whenever I see them."

The judge decided that it would be best if Hans went home before he bashed anyone else. So he paid Hans for the honey himself and Hans went home happy.

## King Midas has Donkey's Ears

In the time of ancient Greece, King Midas made the mistake of offending Apollo, the sun god, so the god gave him donkey's ears as a punishment. King Midas hid his ears under a turban so no one saw them, except his hairdresser, who promised to keep it secret. One day, however, the hairdresser was eager to tell the secret, so he went to a field, dug a hole and whispered it to the earth.

Soon after, a bed of reeds grew up. A musician came and made a pipe out of one of the reeds. He went to King Midas' court and when he played his pipe it sang out, "King Midas has donkey's ears". It was a secret no longer, so King Midas took off his turban at long last.

# Rapunzel

**M**any years ago a husband and wife were expecting their first baby. They were very poor and often hungry. One morning, the woman looked over her garden wall into her neighbour's vegetable patch. There she saw a bed of delicious-looking salad. She longed for it so much that her husband climbed over to get her some.

Unfortunately, their neighbour was an evil witch, who caught him in the act of stealing. The witch would only let the man go if he promised to give her his child.

So when the couple's little daughter was born, the witch took her. She called the girl Rapunzel, and placed her in a high tower with no door in the middle of a forest. As years went by Rapunzel grew into a lovely young woman with golden hair so long and thick that the witch could use it to climb up into the tower.

One day, a prince was riding through the forest. He spotted the witch as she arrived to visit Rapunzel. The prince hid so the witch didn't see the him, and watched as she cried out: "Rapunzel! Rapunzel! Let down your hair!" The golden braid came tumbling out of the window and the witch climbed up. The prince waited till the witch had left, then called out the same words and climbed up himself.

Rapunzel was enchanted to meet the prince, and they soon fell in love. The prince began to plan Rapunzel's escape, and every day he returned with strands of silk, for Rapunzel to weave into a ladder.

One day, the witch noticed a flower that the prince had brought Rapunzel, so she knew someone had visited. She was furious! Grabbing a pair of scissors, she cut off Rapunzel's braid. Then the witch used magic to send Rapunzel to a faraway desert, while she waited in the tower for the prince.

When the prince arrived, the witch let down the braid at his call – and as he neared the top she let go! As the prince hit the ground a crack formed in the tower. It crumbled to the ground with the witch inside.

Somehow the prince survived the fall. Bruised and battered, he set off to look for Rapunzel. At last he came to the desert where she had been banished.

When Rapunzel saw him she threw her arms around him, crying tears of joy. The prince led Rapunzel back to his kingdom – where they lived happily ever after.

# My Own Self

A poor widow once lived with her son in a tiny house. One stormy night, the widow knew that fairies would be up to mischief so she told her son to go bed, but he refused. After the widow went to bed, a tiny girl with wings dropped down the chimney.

"Oh!" said the boy, "What do they call you?"

"My own self," she said, "What do they call you?"

"Just my own self too!" And they began to play together – the fairy made animals, houses and people out of the ashes. As the boy watched, he stirred the coals to make them blaze, and a hot cinder fell on the fairy's tiny foot.

She squealed so loudly that the boy ran upstairs and hid in his bed.

Then a sharp voice came from the chimney, "Who's there, and what's wrong?" it said.

"It's my own self," sobbed the fairy, "and my foot's burnt. Oh how it hurts!"

"Who did it?" said the voice angrily.

"Just my own self too!" said the fairy.

"If you did it your own self," cried the fairy-mother, "why make all this fuss?" And she reached down, grabbed her daughter by the ear, and pulled her up the chimney.

The next evening, the boy's mother was surprised to find that he was happy to go to bed when she asked!

# Mischievous Puck

There was once a very naughty spirit called Puck, who liked to play tricks on people for fun.

One day, he became a fly and listened to a conversation between a couple who were about to be married.

"Oh no!" said the woman, "I have forgotten to buy thread for my wedding dress!"

Just as she spoke these words a large ball of thread appeared by the side of the road. It was beautiful, and made up of every colour you could think of. The man picked it up and took it to the dressmaker, who was delighted with it. It matched the dress perfectly.

The wedding day arrived, and a great crowd assembled to witness the ceremony. The doors were opened, and the bride could be seen from afar.

"What a lovely dress!" whispered everyone. But just as she entered the church… *Crick! Crack! Crick! Crack!* And the wedding dress fell to the ground.

Cloaks were offered to the young bride, and the wedding continued, but she was very upset.

When the dress was examined later it was found that the thread had vanished! But nobody knew that it was all thanks to mischievous Puck!

# The Cat Maiden

**V**enus, **the goddess of beauty,** was debating with the great god Zeus about whether it was possible for a living thing to change its natural habits and instincts. Zeus said yes, it was, but Venus said it was impossible.

To test the question, Zeus turned a cat into a maiden, and arranged for her to get married. When the young couple sat down to the wedding feast, Zeus said, "See how perfectly she behaves. Who could tell that yesterday she was a cat? Surely her nature has changed?"

"Wait," replied Venus, and she conjured up a mouse. Immediately the bride tried to pounce upon it. "Ah, you see," said Venus. "You will have to agree that I am right after all!"

# Paddy Corcoran's Wife

**P**addy Corcoran's wife had been poorly for many years. She lay bedridden, trying medicines of all sorts, until Paddy was nearly brought to despair.

Then one day, a tiny fairy woman dressed in a neat red cloak came in, and said, "Kitty Corcoran, you've had a long lie of it there on your back for seven years, and you're as far from being cured as ever."

"Yes" said Kitty, "that's what I was just thinking about."

"It's your own fault," said the little woman. "All the time you've been ill, your children have thrown out your dirty water after dusk at the very time us fairies are passing your door, which we do every day. Now, if you avoid this and throw it out in a different place, at a different time, the sickness will leave you." The tiny fairy woman then disappeared. Kitty did as she was asked, and the next day she found herself in perfect health once more — to the delight of her husband.

# The Vixen and the Lioness

A lioness and a vixen were talking about their young, as mothers often do.

"My children are the picture of health," said the vixen, proudly.

"Well, my child has a particularly splendid coat," said the lioness, "and his mane is clearly going to be quite a sight to see."

"Everyone tells me how my children are the image of their parents," said the vixen.

"And I am often told that my son is clearly going to be as strong as his father," insisted the lioness.

"It's an absolute joy to see my cubs playing together," said the vixen, then she added, "but I notice you never have more than one."

"That's true," said the lioness with a steely glint in her eye, "but that one grows up to be the King of the Beasts."

# The Old Woman and her Pig

**A**n old woman bought a pig from the market. On her way home she came to a stile, but the pig would not jump over it. The woman saw a dog and had an idea. "Dog! Bite pig," she said. "Pig won't jump over the stile."

The dog wouldn't bite, however, so she went a little further, and found a stick. She said, "Stick! Poke dog – dog won't bite pig and pig won't jump over the stile!" But the stick wouldn't do as she asked either! She travelled on and met a fire, but the fire wouldn't burn the stick. Then she met some water, but the water wouldn't quench the fire. Next she met a horse, but the horse wouldn't drink the water. She went a little further, and she met a rope – but the rope wouldn't lasso the horse. And the little rat she met next wouldn't gnaw the rope!

But then she came across a cat and said, "Cat! Cat! Scare rat."

"All right," said the cat, "if you get me some milk."

The old woman fetched a saucer of milk at once, and after the cat had had a drink, it scared the rat, then the rat gnawed the rope, the rope lassoed the horse, the horse drank the water, the water put out the fire, the fire burnt the stick, the stick beat the dog, the dog bit the pig, the pig jumped over the stile – and that is how the old woman got home before midnight!

# The Fox and the Mask

There was once a fox who got into the storeroom of a
theatre. He examined the scenery, costumes and props,
wondering what everything was.

The fox was delighted when he came across what looked
like a leg of chicken and a hunk of cheese, but when he bit
into them — yuk! He found they were only made of paper
and glue. As he turned to see if he could find any real food,
the fox saw a face grinning down at him. He sprang back
in surprise, but the face didn't move. The fox became a
little bolder and stopped shrinking back — still the face did
not do so much as blink. Then the fox stepped closer — the
face did not flinch. He stuck out his
tongue and blew a raspberry. It
was only a mask, the type
actors use to put over their
faces. "Ah," said the fox, "you
look very fine. It's a pity you
don't have any brains.
Outside show is a poor
substitute for inner worth."

# Nasreddin Hodja and the Tax Collector

One day, a tax collector fell into the river. He didn't know how to swim so the villagers gathered by the riverbank trying to save him.

"Give me your hand, give me your hand," they were all shouting. But the man did not hold out his hand, and it was then that time Nasreddin Hodja walked by.

"Help!" said the villagers, "the tax collector is going to drown. He won't give us his hand."

"Let me try," said Nasreddin. "Here, you," he yelled to the man, "Take my hand!" The tax collector immediately held out his hand and grabbed Nasreddin Hodja's arm. The people around then pulled him out of the water.

"You see," Nasreddin Hodja explained, "You said, 'Give me your hand.' I said, 'Take my hand.' He is a tax collector — he is much better at taking than giving."

# The Young Giant

**M**any years ago, a farmer and his wife had a son who was no bigger than your thumb, called Tiny Tom.

One day Tom was helping his dad in the fields when along came a giant. The giant scooped up Tiny Tom and took him home. For six years the giant fed Tiny Tom huge meals, until he too became huge and strong.

When Tiny Tom returned to his parents, they were amazed to find that he was now a giant. His mother couldn't cook enough food to satisfy enormous appetite. Tiny Tom decided that he couldn't ask his parents to keep him, so he set off to seek his fortune.

Eventually Tiny Tom came to a farm where the farmer was looking for a chief woodcutter. "How much do you want as pay?" the farmer asked.

To his astonishment, Tiny Tom replied, "Nothing. But after I have worked for you for a year, you must let me give you a kick."

The farmer thought Tom must be very stupid, but he agreed at once. He was a greedy man, so he was very pleased that he would not have to pay the giant.

Early the next morning, all the farmhands started getting ready to go into the woods to chop down trees but Tom stayed in bed until midday. Then he spent several hours consuming a huge breakfast. By the time he entered the forest the other workers were on their way home, leading horses that pulled carts full of logs they had cut.

In a matter of minutes Tiny Tom ripped ten trees out of the earth, tossed them like matchsticks into a cart, and pulled it back to the farm much faster than any horse could. He even overtook the other workers on the way. The greedy farmer was delighted.

Tiny Tom served the farmer for a whole year – and then, when the other workers were getting their wages, it was time for him to have his kick.

"Stand still," he said to the farmer. Then, with barely a tap of his enormous boot, the farmer flew high up into the air and where he landed nobody knows.

But what I can tell you is that Tiny Tom took over the farm and became the most successful, happiest farmer for miles around.

# The Greedy Brownie

There was once a brownie who loved playing tricks, as most brownies do. One day, he passed a dairy and thought it would be a good place to rest.

But his sleep was soon disturbed by two girls, called Jean and Meg, who had come to steal a taste of the cream with a ladle. This gave the naughty brownie an idea!

He crept up behind the girls and blew out their candle so they had to drink in the dark. Then, as Jean lifted the ladle, the brownie lapped up all the cream before it reached her mouth. Meg snatched the ladle and tried to have her turn, but the brownie once again got there first. Jean snatched back the ladle from Meg. On it went, until the brownie was full of cream — the girls didn't get a drop!

Just then the farmer's wife entered. She believed the girls were the culprits and scolded them for their naughtiness, while the little brownie ran away laughing.

# Cinderella

Long ago, a girl called Cinderella lived in a grand house with her father, her stepmother and her two stepsisters. Her step-mother was a bad-tempered woman, who made Cinderella work like a servant, while her own daughters were treated like royalty.

One day, news arrived from the king that a ball was to be held for the prince. Every young lady in the country was to be invited so that the prince could choose a bride.

The stepsisters were delighted and immediately started to order Cinderella about, with cries of, "Brush my hair!" and "Iron my dress!" When they were ready, they flounced off with their stepmother to the palace, leaving Cinderella behind.

Just as Cinderella began to despair, a friendly-looking old woman appeared from nowhere, and said, "Don't cry, Cinderella. I'm your fairy godmother and you shall go to the ball. Just be back by midnight — the spell ends when the clock chimes twelve."

With a click of her fingers the old woman changed Cinderella's rags into a beautiful golden dress. Then in a flash she turned a pumpkin from the vegetable patch into a carriage. Cinderella climbed inside and it set off.

When she arrived at the palace the prince was immediately enchanted. He took Cinderella by the hand and danced with her all night. She looked so different that no one recognized her, not even her family.

Cinderella danced with the prince all night. It was nearly midnight when she slipped away. In her haste she lost one of her shoes on the castle steps as she ran.

The prince was determined to find the lovely stranger, and the very next day he set out to find the girl the shoe fitted.

He went from house to house, but no one could squeeze a foot into the dainty shoe. The prince was losing hope when he arrived at Cinderella's house. The stepsisters tried and tried but neither could force their foot into the slipper. "Do you have any other daughters?" the prince asked Cinderella's stepmother.

At that moment Cinderella entered the room. Of course the shoe fitted her perfectly.

"I've found my bride!" the prince cried. A grand wedding was arranged, and they lived happily ever after.

# The Days of the Week

The days of the week decided to have a fancy-dress party, just for fun.

Sunday came dressed up as a priest about to go to church. Monday was a schoolboy because school starts on Monday. Tuesday was a warrior holding a sword in his hand. "Tuesday comes from the name of the Viking god of combat, Tyr," he explained. Wednesday turned up as a prince, with a golden crown on his head. Thursday also dressed as a warrior. "I am named after the Viking god of thunder, Thor," he said. Friday came dressed in a long robe. "My name comes from the Viking goddess of love, Freya," she smiled. Saturday dressed as a housewife and brought a big plate of sandwiches with her. Then the party got under way — and a very good time they had too!

# Pandora's Box

**L**ong ago in Greece, the god Zeus made the first woman. He gave her the gifts of wisdom, kindness and beauty, and named her Pandora, which means 'All-gifts'. Zeus gave her a sealed box, and he warned her never to open it.

Pandora lived happily, but the thought of the sealed box nagged at her mind. One day, she decided to open it, just a crack. As she lifted the lid, swarming, biting creatures — all sorts of evil and misery — rushed out.

Pandora slammed the box shut, but it was too late. She was overcome with sadness at what she had let out into the world.

But then she glanced into what she thought was the empty box, and saw that one creature remained. It was hope — the one thing that keeps people going when times are bad. So Pandora also let hope out into the world.

# The Bremen Town Musicians

**A** **donkey, a cat, a dog and a cockerel** left their homes and decided to go to Bremen to become musicians.

It was too far to walk in one day to reach the town that evening, so as night fell they looked for a place to sleep. Soon they came to a little house. The donkey went to the window and looked in.

"My goodness," he gasped. "There's all sorts of good things to eat and drink — but there is a gang of robbers inside!"

The animals stood on each other's shoulders to get a look, but they overbalanced and crashed through the window, making a terrible racket. The frightened robbers took flight, and as soon as they

were gone the animals made themselves comfortable and went to sleep.

But the youngest robber crept back to see what had caused the noise. Nervously, he tiptoed up to the house and gently pushed open the door. He went to light a match from the coals and at once the cat flew in his face, spitting and scratching. The robber ran to the back door, but the dog sprang up and bit him on the leg. He leapt outside, where the donkey gave him a kick with its hind foot. Then the cockerel, which had been awakened by the noise, cried down from a beam in the roof, "Cockadoodledooooo!"

The youngest robber ran back to his captain as fast as he could, and said, "There is a horrible witch sitting in the house, who scratched my face with her long claws. By the back door stood a man with a knife who stabbed me in the leg. In the yard lies a monster who beat me with a wooden club. And above, on the roof, sat a ghost who screeched and wailed!"

After this the robbers never dared go back to the house again. But it suited the animals so well that they lived there happily for the rest of their days.

# The Two Soldiers and the Robber

**Two soldiers were** walking along a road when they were set upon by a robber. One soldier ran away, but the other put up such a fight that the robber himself bolted.

When the coast was clear, the first soldier returned, yelling, "Where is he? Let me at him."

The brave soldier replied, "You are a little late, my friend. Calm yourself, and put away your weapon. It is no good pretending to be brave after the event."

# The Mischievous Dog

**A man once had a dog** that barked and snapped at all his visitors. The man found this a nuisance. He tied a bell around the dog's neck so people approaching his house would hear the dog and stay back.

The dog was proud of the bell and strutted about, as if he were wearing a medal. An old dog came up to him and said, "You don't think, do you, that your bell was given as a reward? No, it is a badge of disgrace."

# In Times of Danger

Three fish, whose names were Plan Ahead, Think Fast, and Wait and See lived in a pond. They heard a man plan to fish in their pond the next day.

Plan Ahead said, "I'm swimming away tonight."

Think Fast said, "I'll come up with a plan."

Wait and See lazily said, "I can't think about it now."

When the fisherman cast his nets, Plan Ahead was long gone. But Think Fast and Wait and See were both caught! Think Fast pretended to be dead so the fisherman threw him back. But Wait and See ended up at the fish market!

# The Two Jewels

A mighty king of India once said to his admiring servants, "Whoever can walk round my kingdom in the shortest time shall have one of these two jewels." One

of the servants stood up, walked round the king, and said, "Sir, may I have the prize?"

"Why?" said the king.

"Why, you are the kingdom, are you not?" said the courtier.

The king was so pleased with his answer that he gave him both the jewels.

# The Donkey and its Shadow

**Y**ears ago a man was going on a long journey, so he hired a donkey to carry his luggage. The donkey's owner said he would load the animal, and be the driver.

They set off down the road, making good progress until the sun blazed overhead and they stopped to rest.

The traveller wanted to lie in the donkey's shadow, but the owner wouldn't let him — he said he had hired the donkey, not its shadow. The quarrel grew heated and, while the men were fighting, the donkey shed its cargo, took to its heels and was soon out of sight!

# The Three Wishes

**A** poor fisherman lived by the edge of the sea in a tumbledown old cottage with his wife, who was always grumbling.

One evening he caught a tiny fish. "Please throw me back into the sea," said the fish, "and I will grant you the first three wishes made in your cottage."

The fisherman ran all the way home in great excitement to tell his wife about the tiny fish.

"Whoever heard of talking a fish?" snapped his wife as she slammed down a plate of dry bread.

"I wish this was a plate of fine sausages, for I am so hungry," said the fisherman wistfully.

No sooner were the words out of his mouth than there in front of him was a plate of sizzling sausages! But instead of being pleased, his wife yelled, "Why couldn't you have wished for something better? We could have had chests of gold! You old fool! I wish the sausages were at the end of your nose!"

Immediately the sausages were stuck on his nose. The fisherman and his wife pulled and pulled at the sausages, but it was no good. They were stuck fast. There was nothing for it, they would have to use the last wish.

"I wish the sausages would disappear," said the fisherman sadly, and they did in a flash. So there they sat, the poor fisherman and his grumbling wife. No delicious supper of sizzling sausages and, much worse, no magic wishes. The fisherman never caught the tiny fish again, and his wife never stopped grumbling.

# The Delicious Soup

**O**nce **upon a time** there was a poor little girl who often went hungry at home. Then one day she met an old woman, who gave her a magic pot. If you said, "Boil, little pot!" it cooked delicious soup, and it only stopped when you said, "Stop, little pot!" The little girl took the pot home, so her family could have good soup whenever they liked.

One day the little girl went out, and her mother said, "Boil, little pot!" She ate all she wanted, but when she wanted it to stop, she forgot the magic words. The soup filled the kitchen, then the house, and soon the whole street. Finally, the child returned and said at once: "Stop, little pot!"

Immediately it stopped — but whoever wishes to enter the village must now swim through the soup!

# The Peacock and Hera

A long, long time ago, in the early days of the world, the gods and goddesses of Mount Olympus ruled over earth, sky and sea.

At this time there was a peacock who prayed earnestly to the goddess Hera, Queen of Mount Olympus. The peacock was more than happy with his beautiful looks, which all the other birds envied, but he longed to have a better singing voice to go with it. He had quite an ugly cry, and what he really wanted was the voice of a nightingale.

However, the great Hera refused. The peacock would not take no for an answer and continued to beg. "Please grant me this," he pleaded, "after all, I am your favourite bird."

But Hera just replied, "Be content with what you have — no one can be best at everything."

# Mother Holle

There was once a woman who made her stepdaughter do all the chores, while her own daughter did nothing.

The stepdaughter was going about her work one day when she dropped a spindle into the well. Fearing her stepmother's anger, she jumped in to rescue it. But instead of landing in the water she found herself in a meadow.

She walked along a path until she met an old woman. The woman said, "I'm Mother Holle. Stay with me and you will be rewarded. You must shake out my pillows every day, for that makes it snow on earth."

The girl stayed and worked hard, but she missed her home. Mother Holle led her to a door, and as she walked out, a shower of gold pieces fell on her. "That is your reward for working so hard," Mother Holle explained, and she showed the girl her way home.

The girl's greedy stepmother was amazed to see her covered in gold. She ordered her own daughter to get some gold too, and pushed her down the well.

On the first day at Mother Holle's house, the girl toiled hard, but by the second day she was her usual lazy self. Mother Holle told her to go home. The girl thought of the gold, and was pleased. But as she stood beneath the doorway, a shower of black tar poured all over her. "That's your reward," said Mother Holle, as she shut the door.

# The Master and his Pupil

A clever man had a big black book, which he had forbidden his pupil to touch. One day, when his master was out, the lad sneaked into the master's study to look at the book. He opened it and read one line out loud.

A loud clap of thunder rolled through the room and there stood a terrible monster.

"Set me a task!" it roared.

"Water the flower!" cried the lad in panic, pointing to a geranium. The monster brought water and poured it onto the flower — but he did not stop. Soon the floor was covered with water. "Enough, enough!" gasped the lad. But the monster took no notice. The water rose to the lad's knees, to his waist, to his chin. Suddenly, the master rushed in and spoke the words to end the spell. And he never left his book unlocked again.

# The Wise Mamad who Always Told the Truth

**O**nce upon a time there lived a wise man called Mamad, who never lied. The king heard about him and decided to play a trick.

The king held his horse by the reins, placed his left foot on the stirrup and told Mamad to tell the queen he was going hunting. Mamad bowed and left. Then the king laughed, and said, "We won't go hunting and so Mamad will have lied."

But wise Mamad went to the queen and said, "The king said he was going hunting but I don't know if he finished mounting his horse after I left."

Then the next day the king told the queen, "The wise Mamad lied to you yesterday."

But the queen told him what Mamad had said, and the king realized that the wise man only tells what he has actually seen.

# The Lion and the Boar

**A** **lion and a boar** came to a spring one morning. They argued over who should be the first to drink.

"I was here first," growled the boar.

"Not so," insisted the lion, "I arrived before you."

The quarrel continued, until the lion and the boar suddenly charged at one another. They fought furiously until, pausing to take a breath, they saw some vultures seated nearby. The beady-eyed birds were obviously waiting for one of them to be killed so they could feed.

"If you're thinking what I'm thinking," said the lion, "we'd better make up."

"Yes," agreed the boar, "I'd rather forget our quarrel and live, than be food for vultures."

# Why the Manx Cat has no Tail

Noah had nearly finished leading all the animals into the ark when a cat decided that she would like to go mousing one last time.

Noah's wife called and called her, but she would not come. Cats are always contrary!

Noah began to shut the door, but just then up pranced the cat. She just managed to slip through the gap, but her tail was caught in the door as it slammed shut. The cat was very cross as her tail was cut off, but Noah told her it was her own fault.

Forty days later, the flood was over and Noah opened the door of the ark once more. First out was the cat, and she ran and ran until she found the Isle of Man, and there she stopped. Ever since then, cats from the Isle of Man have had no tails.

# The Fish and the Hare

**O**nce upon a time, a man found a pot of gold between some trees.

'Oh, what luck!' he thought. 'But I can't take it home because my wife will tell the whole world!'

He made a plan. He bought a pike and a hare at the market. Then he returned to the forest and tied the pike to a tree and the hare to a reed by a stream. Then he trotted home to tell his wife about what he had found.

They set off to retrieve the pot and it wasn't long before the couple came across the pike flapping at the top of the tree and the hare wriggling by the water. The wife was flabbergasted. They dug up the pot and drove home.

Now the old couple had plenty of money. But the wife was foolish, and told everyone about it. The governor of the town decided to take the couple's riches for himself, so he sent his secretary to tell the man to give it to him.

But the old man just shrugged his shoulders and said, "What treasure? Pardon me, but my wife is not in her right mind, sir. Ask her how it happened."

"We were driving through the forest," cried the wife, "and we saw a pike at home in the top of a tree and a hare in the stream—"

"What rubbish!" shouted the secretary, as he left. So the clever old man got to keep his money to himself.

# The Cat Mill

**O**nce upon a time, a troll lived on a hill above a mill. Every evening he would enter the mill and demand a large glass of beer, which he would drink noisily, while shouting loudly and throwing the flour sacks around.

One night a travelling bear trainer took shelter for the night in the mill with his bears. The troll arrived as usual and jumped onto the bears, thinking they would be easy to attack. However, they scratched him so badly that he was barely able to escape!

The troll never entered the mill again but one day, looking down from the hilltop, he saw the miller and shouted, "Miller, do you still have those mean cats?"

And that is how the mill came to be known as the Cat Mill.

# The Dog and the Wolf

It was a hot day on the farm, and the sleepy dog was on guard at the gate. He tried to stay awake but it was no good. Just as his eyes shut a wolf pounced and suddenly, the dog was fighting for his life.

He begged for mercy, saying, "Wolf, I will make a wretched meal. But if you wait a few days, my master is giving a feast. The leftovers will be mine and I shall get nice and fat. That will be a better time to eat me." So the wolf let him go and sloped away.

As the dog had said, the feast took place and he ate his fill of tasty leftovers. The next day, the wolf arrived, only to find the dog out of reach on the stable roof.

"My friend," the dog said, "if you catch me down there again, don't wait for any feast."

# Brabo and the Giant

**Years ago,** a giant lived on the banks of the river that flowed through Antwerp in Belgium. Every day, hundreds of ships sailed on the river, trading goods and making the city wealthy.

But one day, the giant built a castle on the riverbank with dark, damp dungeons. With a big knotted club, he strode through the town. "From this day," he roared, "no ship shall pass by this place without paying me."

The people were terrified, and for a time they did as the giant said. The giant grew rich and the city became poor. After a few months a brave young fellow named Brabo spotted a window where he could climb into the giant's chamber. Brabo went to the duke and promised that he would seek out the giant if his soldiers would storm the gates of the giant's castle and distract him.

The duke agreed and hundreds of men marched against the gates. At the same time, Brabo climbed into the castle and snuck up on the giant, who had rushed to see the men at the gates. Brave Brabo threw an enormous net and at last the giant was captured.

That night every window of every house in Antwerp showed lighted candles to celebrate, and the city was bathed in light.

# The Important Thing

A scholar, who studied many books, asked a boatman to row him across a river. As they started, the scholar said, "Tell me, boatman, what use you've made of your life. Have you ever studied history or science?'"

"No," said the boatman.

"Have you learnt languages? Or mathematics?"

"No," said the boatman, "not at all."

"Too bad," said the scholar, "Learning is the most important thing. You've wasted half your life."

Suddenly the rickety boat crashed into a rock in the middle of the river. The boatman turned to the scholar and said, "Wise man, tell me, have you ever learnt to swim?"

"No," said the scholar, "I've spent my life thinking."

"Too bad," said the boatman, "You've wasted your life. For now the boat is sinking."

# The Eagle and the Beetle

**A**n eagle was once hunting a hare, who was running for her life. As the hare sprinted, she saw a beetle and gasped for help. Although the beetle was tiny, he agreed. Sadly the eagle still caught the hare, but from then on whenever the eagle laid an egg, the beetle rolled it out of the nest.

After a few years of this, the eagle went to the god Jupiter for help. Jupiter allowed the eagle to lay her eggs in his lap, where they would be safe. But the beetle had a plan. He made a ball of dirt the size of an eagle's egg, and placed it on top of the eggs in the god's lap. When Jupiter saw the dirt, he stood up to shake it out of his robe, and shook out the eggs too! Ever since then, eagles never lay their eggs in the season when beetles are about.

# The Accomplished
# and Lucky Teakettle

**A** long time ago in Japan there was an old teakettle in a
temple. One day, when the temple priest was about to
hang it over the hearth to boil some water, the kettle
suddenly sprouted the head and tail of a badger. What a
wonderful kettle! It danced all over the room, and was
impossible to catch.

But soon the priest found the kettle too much trouble
and sold it to a tinker. The tinker was astounded to find
that the accomplished teakettle could dance and walk a
tightrope.

The tinker displayed the
kettle in an exhibition that
travelled the country.
Everyone came to see it, even
princesses and the emperor!
The tinker soon grew so rich
that he gave the kettle back to
the temple, where it was put
on show as a precious
treasure and worshipped as
a saint.

# The Dog, the Cat and the Mice

**I**n the beginning the cat and dog were friendly with each other, each doing their own work.

But then they drew up an agreement. They decided the dog would do the outside work, and the cat would do the work inside. Once it was settled upon, the cat put the agreement in the loft.

Everything was going well until one day the dog said he didn't see why he had to protect the house and get cold, whilst the cat was comfortable inside.

The cat said, "We had an agreement."

The dog replied, "Let me see it."

So the cat went up to the loft, but mice had eaten the agreement and it was just a heap of fluff.

The cat was furious and chased the mice away. When the cat told the dog that she didn't have the agreement, the dog growled at her. Since that time, whenever a dog meets a cat he asks her for the agreement, and as she cannot show it to him, he growls. And the cat, knowing the mice ate the agreement, runs after them whenever she sees them.

# The Horse, Hunter and Stag

**A** horse and a stag were great friends, but one day, they quarrelled badly and the friendship ended.

The horse decided to seek revenge, so he asked a hunter for help. The hunter listened as the horse explained how he wanted him to scare away the stag. "I will help you," the hunter said, "but to be successful, you must let me ride you."

The horse agreed, and the hunter soon saddled and bridled him. With the horse's speed, the hunter chased down the stag and scared it. The delighted horse thanked him. Then he said, "Now remove those things from my mouth and back."

"Not so fast," said the hunter. "Now I have you I will keep you."

# Nasreddin Hodja is Caught in a Lie

One day Nasreddin Hodja's neighbour came to him and said, "Nasreddin, we need a donkey for a few hours. Can I borrow yours?"

Nasreddin did not want to lend his donkey, so he thought quickly. Then he said, "I would gladly help, dear neighbour, but he is not here at the moment."

Just then the donkey's loud and long bray was heard from the shed.

"Shame on you," said the neighbour, "I've caught you out in a lie — your donkey is braying in his shed."

"My dear fellow," Nasreddin Hodja said calmly, "are you going to believe my word or are you going to believe a donkey?"

# The Old Man and the Fairies

**M**any years ago, when the Welsh mountains were full of fairies, an old man was walking to a market. On the way he sat down to rest in a lonely valley, and dropped off into a deep sleep.

While he slept, the fairies came and carried him off under the earth. He awoke after a while and found himself in a great palace of gold, filled with fairies dancing and singing. At the end of the night the fairies carried the man back to the valley, and when he looked in his bag he found it filled with gold! The man just managed to pick it up, and stagger home with it. His wife came out to greet him, and said, "Where have you been?"

He explained what had happened and showed her the gold. They agreed to go and spend it the very next day, but in the morning they found the bag was in fact full of cockleshells!

# Snow White and the Seven Dwarfs

**O**nce upon a time there was a princess called Snow White, whose stepmother, the queen, was both beautiful and cruel.

The queen owned a magic mirror, which could answer questions. The queen would ask, "Who is the fairest in the land?" And the mirror would always reply, "You are, O Queen." But as Snow White grew up she became more lovely than her stepmother, and one day this was the mirror's answer to the queen's question.

Outraged, the queen ordered one of her huntsmen to take Snow White into the forest and abandon her. Poor Snow White wandered for hours. At last she came to the house of seven dwarfs, who kindly took her in and let her live with them. Every day the dwarfs went off to work, and told Snow White not to open the door to anyone, in case the queen came looking for her.

Then one day the queen asked the mirror her usual question, and the mirror told the queen that Snow White was still the fairest and living in the woods.

The queen simmered with fury! The next morning, she disguised herself as an old apple-seller and filled one of her apples with a strong sleeping potion. Then she walked through the forest and found the little cottage where Snow White lived happily with the dwarfs.

The queen waited until the dwarfs had left for work, and then she strode towards the cottage crying, "Apples, delicious apples for sale!"

Snow White looked out of the window, but she did not open the door. The queen saw her and came to the window. "Look how ripe and beautiful they are. I'll take a bite of this one, to show you." She bit into the side with no potion, and held the apple out to Snow White.

Snow White couldn't resist. She took one bite, and fell to the floor as though she would never wake again. The queen returned home, very pleased with her day's work.

The dwarfs returned home and were unable to wake their beloved Snow White. Overcome with sadness, they made a beautiful glass box, and laid Snow White in it. They set the box in a beautiful glade.

Soon after, a prince came riding by and saw the beautiful sleeping princess. He asked

the dwarfs if he could try to wake her and they agreed. As the prince's servants lifted the box up, one of them stumbled and Snow White received such a jolt that the apple flew out of her throat. She began to breathe again!

It was love at first sight for the prince and Snow White, and they lived happily ever after.

And the queen was so angry that her plan didn't work that she disappeared in a puff of smoke, never to be seen again.

# The Foolish Wise Man

A wise man, a bald man and a barber were once travelling together. They stopped for the night and agreed to take turns keeping watch as it was a dangerous part of the country. It was the barber's turn first. He propped up the sleeping wise man, and, for a joke, shaved his head. When it was the wise man's turn to keep watch the barber woke him up. The wise man felt his bare head and shouted loudly at the barber, "What a fool you are! You have woken the bald man instead of me!" Perhaps he wasn't so wise after all!

# The Mice that Ate some Iron Scales

**L**ong ago there was a man who had only a pair of valuable iron scales in his possession. He left them with a merchant for safekeeping while he travelled. When he returned, the man asked for his scales, but the merchant said, "They have been eaten by mice."

The man knew this was a trick and he was angry. He went off, sneaking the merchant's little boy with him. The merchant followed him to his house and said, "Where is my son?"

The man said, "A hawk carried him off."

The merchant replied, "That's impossible."

The man said, "If mice can eat iron, a hawk can carry a boy."

When the merchant heard this, he knew he was found out. He gave the man back his scales, and the man returned the merchant's son.

# Why the Tail of the Fox has a White Tip

**A**n old **woman was looking** for a shepherd to watch her sheep when she met a fox.

"I will watch your sheep for you," said the cunning fox. And he went to work.

At the end of each day, however, one of the sheep was missing. "Where is my sheep?" the woman would ask and the fox would answer, "The wolf ate it."

One day the woman thought, 'Mr Fox must feel guilty. I'll take him a drink of cream.' She went to the field, and caught the fox attacking a sheep! "You cunning fox!" she cried.

The woman had nothing to throw at him but the cream, so she threw that. It struck the tip of his tail, and from that day to this, the tip of the fox's tail has been as white as cream.

# The Hare-brained Crocodiles

**L**ong, long ago, in Japan, on the island of Oki, there lived a little white hare. The hare was bored with life on the tiny island and wanted very much to cross over to the mainland. One day as usual, the hare was standing on the beach, looking towards the mainland when he saw a great crocodile swimming nearby. 'This is lucky!' thought the hare. 'I will ask the crocodile to carry me across the sea!'

But the hare knew that crocodiles could be dangerous so he thought of a trick.

He said, "Oh, Mr Crocodile, I know very little about you. Won't you come out of the sea and play on the shore?"

The crocodile had been feeling quite lonely, so he agreed.

"Tell me, do you think there are more crocodiles than hares?" said the hare, after a while.

"Of course, there are," answered the crocodile haughtily. "Can you not see that for yourself?"

So the hare said, "Do you think there are so many crocodiles that it is possible for you to call up enough to form a line across the sea to the mainland?"

The crocodile snorted and answered, "Of course."

"Then do try," said the artful hare, "and I will count them!"

The crocodile went off and reappeared, bringing with him many more crocodiles.

"Look, Mr Hare," announced the crocodile proudly. "There are enough crocodiles to stretch from here as far as India!" Then the whole company of crocodiles arranged themselves so as to form a bridge between the island of Oki and the mainland.

The hare hopped off the island on to the bridge of crocodiles, saying, "Now I'll count you," as he jumped from one crocodile to the next. "One, two, three, four, five, six, seven…" And so the cunning hare hopped right across the crocodiles to the mainland!

# The Farmyard Cockerel and the Weathervane

**O**nce upon a time, there was a weathervane on top of a farmhouse. Although he was so rusty that he no longer turned with the wind, he was very proud of his high position. He looked down on the hens, chicks and a fine cockerel in the yard below.

"Cockadoodledoo!" the farmyard cockerel crowed. "My chicks will grow up big and strong, just like their father," and he flapped his wings and crowed again.

"That cockerel is stupid," said the haughty weathervane. "What is he good for? He can't even lay an egg!"

But then there came a mighty gust of wind and the weathervane snapped right off. His rusty old fixings had broken. He tumbled to the ground and had to lie there while the birds pecked and scratched around him.

# Odds and Ends

There was a girl who was pretty but very lazy. If, when she was spinning, there was a little knot in the flax, she would pull out a big hunk, and throw it away. She had a hard-working servant, however, who gathered the thrown-away bits of flax, spun them fine, and made beautiful dresses from the waste.

Now, the lazy girl was due to be married, and on the night before the wedding, there was a great party. The servant girl looked very beautiful, dancing in one of her dresses. As they watched, the bride said to her husband-to-be, "Look at her, all dressed in my odds and ends."

When the man asked the girl what she meant she explained that her servant was wearing a dress made of discarded flax. When the man heard how lazy his future wife was, he gave her up and asked the servant to marry him instead.

# Chicken Licken

**O**ne fine day an acorn fell on Chicken Licken's head and he panicked, thinking that the sky was falling in. He set off to tell the king. On the way he met Henny Penny, Cocky Locky, Ducky Lucky and Drakey Lakey. They said that they would come with Chicken Licken to see the king. Next they met Goosey Loosey and Turkey Lurkey – they said they would come as well.

A little further down the road they met Foxy Loxy. "We are off to tell the king that the sky is falling in." Chicken Licken clucked importantly.

"I know the way," said Foxy Loxy with a cunning smile. "Follow me."

So they all set off behind Foxy Loxy. He led them straight to his den where he ate them all up! So the king never heard that the sky was falling in (which it wasn't, of course).

# The Poor Miller's Boy and the Cat

An old miller wished to retire, so one day he said to his three servants, "I will give the mill to whoever brings me the best horse."

So they all set off. Two of the men decided to team up and left the third, who was called Eric, alone. Trudging along a road on his own, he met a small grey cat. To his great surprise it spoke to him. "If you work as my servant for seven years, I will give you the most beautiful horse in the world."

So Eric went to the grey cat's enchanted castle, which was filled with her cat servants. They sat down to enjoy a meal together, and the grey cat told him his task would be to chop wood every day.

Eric stayed with the cats and worked hard, and was very content there. When the seven years were up, the grey cat said to him, "Go back to the mill, and in three days' time I will bring you a horse."

Eric set off down the road to the mill, where he met the other two servants. They had brought the miller old nags, and they mocked Eric for returning with nothing. But on the third day, a golden coach drove up pulled by six gleaming horses. Behind them, a groom rode upon a seventh. The miller thought this was the best horse he had ever seen, and said at once that Eric would inherit the mill.

Just then the coach came to a stop, and a beautiful princess stepped out. She told Eric, "I was the grey cat. By serving me faithfully for seven years you broke the enchantment upon me!"

So instead of becoming a miller, Eric married the beautiful princess, and the two lived happily ever after.

# The Fairy Fluffikins

The Fairy Fluffikins was the funniest little fairy you ever saw, but she was also very naughty. She tickled the baby dormice until they screamed with laughter, she filled the squirrel's nut stores with pebbles and teased the owl with a dead mouse on a string by pulling it away when he went for it. But one day she got into trouble herself. She was poking about when she found a little house with wire walls and a wooden door. In she hopped, but it was a trap!

There was a bang, the wooden door slammed, and Fluffikins was caught.

In the morning the farmer found her, and carried her home to his little girl. So if you call on Ann Smith you will see Fairy Fluffikins there in a little cage.

# The Lion and the Bull

One day a lion passed by a field of cattle. Among them was a huge bull and the lion began to drool with hunger. He went away and thought hard about how he could get the bull into his clutches.

The next day the lion sent the bull an invitation to come to dinner. The bull was flattered at being asked, and he accepted at once.

That evening the excited bull made his way to the lion's den. The lion told the bull to make himself at home. But the bull looked carefully around him. He noticed at once that there was little sign of anything cooking, and left. The lion called out after him to ask his reason for going. The bull called back, "When I saw your kitchen it struck me at once that dinner was to be a bull."

# The Bat, the Birds and the Beasts

There was a time when the birds and the beasts always argued. After a while the two sides decided to wage war on each other.

When the armies were ready, the bat hesitated about which to join. The birds said, "Come with us."

But the bat said, "I am a beast."

The beasts said, "Join us."

But the bat said, "I am a bird."

Luckily, peace was settled and no battle took place. The bat heard the birds celebrating.

"Can I join in?" he asked, but the birds flew at him angrily.

The beasts were also having a party. The bat again asked to join in and again was driven away.

"I see," said the bat, "I did not say I was one thing or the other, so now I don't fit anywhere."

# The Wise Men of Gotham and the Cuckoo

The foolish wise men of Gotham loved to hear the call of the cuckoo in spring, so one year they decided to try and capture it. They thought that if they kept a bird in the village they could enjoy hearing its call all year round. The foolish men planted a thick hedge in a circle, and wove extra twigs into it to make it far too dense for a cuckoo to fly through. Finally they trapped a cuckoo, and put it inside the ring of hedges.

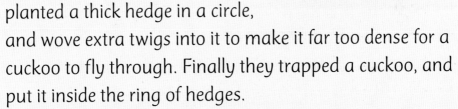

The men stood back proudly, pleased with their work. But of course, the first thing the cuckoo did was fly away up into the sky.

The men of Gotham scratched their heads. "We didn't make the hedge high enough," they said sadly.

# The Three Little Pigs

There were once three little pigs who decided to make their own way in the world. The first little pig set out and built a house of straw, but along came a big bad wolf.

"Little pig, little pig, let me come in!" shouted the big bad wolf.

"No, not by the hair on my chinny chin chin. I'll not let you in," squeaked the first little pig.

"Then I'll huff and I'll puff, and I'll blow your house down," yelled the wolf. And he did. He huffed and he puffed and he blew the straw house down. The first little pig squealed and ran away as fast as she could, before the wolf could catch her.

Meanwhile, the second little pig built a house out of sticks. Along came the big bad wolf. "Little pig, little pig, let me come in!" shouted the wolf.

"No, not by the hair on my chinny chin chin. I'll not let you in," squeaked the second little pig.

"Then I'll huff and I'll puff, and I'll blow your house down," yelled the wolf. And he did. The second little pig escaped just in time.

Now, the third little pig had built a house out of bricks. Along came the big bad wolf. "Little pig, little pig, let me come in!" shouted the wolf.

"No, not by the hair on my chinny chin chin. I'll not let you in," squeaked the third little pig.

"Then I'll huff and I'll puff, and I'll blow your house down," yelled the wolf. And he tried. He huffed and he puffed but he could not blow the brick house down.

So the wolf decided to climb down the chimney, but when he reached the bottom he fell into a big pot of water that the little pig had placed on the fire. Dripping wet and much too hot, the wolf ran away, never to return!

And the little pigs all lived happily together in the little brick house.

# The Toad's Godmother

Two girls were walking along a path when a huge toad waddled in front of them. One of the girls joked that if the toad ever had a baby, she would be its godmother. The other one added that she would cook for the occasion.

A few days later the girls met an old woman who reminded them of their promise, and asked them to come to the baptism of the toad's child. She led them to the toad's house. The first girl was appointed godmother, and the other cooked a fine feast. Then the woman sent them on their way, and gave them a bag of coal.

As they walked, they let most of the coal fall to the ground, as it was quite heavy. But when they got home, they saw that the little bit of coal they still had was pure gold – how they wish they had kept it all!

# The Lion, the Fox and the Beasts

The lion once fell very ill, so he summoned all the animals to him so he could tell them his last wishes.

First, the goat came to the lion's cave.

He was gone a long time, so a sheep decided to go in to see what had happened. When the sheep also did not return, a calf decided to enter the cave to hear the lion's last wishes.

After a while, the lion appeared outside. Strangely, he was feeling stronger. He saw a fox waiting. "Why did you not come to see me?" he snarled.

"I beg your pardon," said the fox, "but I noticed the tracks of the animals that had entered the cave. And while I see many going in, I can't see any coming out. Until all the animals come out, I will stay here."

# The Nightingale

The emperor of China lived in the most splendid palace in the world surrounded by a large, beautiful garden. In the forest nearby there lived a nightingale and all the world praised its song.

When the emperor was told of its beautiful singing he demanded it be brought to him. The nightingale sang sweetly, and the emperor was entranced. He built it a golden cage and listened to its song every day. But one day, the emperor was given a golden clockwork bird encrusted with jewels, that sang when you wound it up. It only had one song that was always the same, but the emperor loved his new toy and didn't notice when the real nightingale flew back to the forest.

Years passed. The emperor fell sick, and it seemed nothing could save him. He begged to hear the golden notes of his toy bird one last time, but when they wound it up, it was found to be broken and couldn't sing.

As the emperor lay in bed, a bird flew in through the window and started to sing. It was the real nightingale, returned to help the man who had loved it once. It sang so sweetly that all the king's sickness passed from him. When the courtiers came in the next morning, the emperor greeted them cheerfully — he was feeling so much better.

# The Donkey and the Old Peasant

**A**n old peasant was on a journey with his donkey, which he was driving along with a stick. All his belongings were strapped to the poor animal's back.

The peasant decided to have a rest when all of a sudden he caught sight of armed men stealthily approaching.

The terrified peasant jumped onto the donkey's back, begging it to run as fast as it could. But the donkey did not budge. It said, "Do you think those men will make me carry heavier loads than I have now?"

"Probably not," said the peasant.

"Oh well," said the donkey, "I don't mind if they do take me, for I shan't be any worse off."

And it returned to nibbling the grass, leaving its master to his fate.

# The Kindness of the Fire God

There once lived a very rich man who set out on a long journey. On the way he met a woman, dressed in red, who begged him to take her with him. The rich man kindly agreed, helped her onto his wagon, and they set off together.

They had not gone far when the woman said, "I am the Fire God. As you are a good man I will give you this warning — tomorrow a fire will break out in your house. Hurry home and save what you can!" With that, she vanished.

The man drove home as fast as he could. Just as he removed the last of his possessions from his house, a fire broke out and raged until the whole building burnt down. The man was thankful for the Fire God's warning!

# The Crow and the Pitcher

There was once a crow who had been unable to find water for many days — not even a drop. Imagine his joy when he suddenly came upon a water pitcher.

However, when the crow put its beak into the mouth of the pitcher he found that he could not reach far enough down to get to the water. He tried and tried, but at last had to give up in despair.

Then a clever thought occurred to him, and he took a pebble and dropped it into the pitcher. The water level rose slightly. Then he took another pebble and dropped it in. Then another, and another…

At last, the crow saw the water rise up near him, and after casting in a few more pebbles he was able to quench his thirst. "Little by little does the trick," he said to himself.

# Nasreddin Hodja and the Delicious Stew

**N**asreddin Hodja brought two kilograms of meat home one day, and asked his wife to cook a nice stew for dinner. Then he went off to work. Nasreddin's wife cooked a stew, but at lunch time a few of her relatives visited. She served them the stew, and they finished it all.

When Nasreddin came home and asked his wife if the stew was ready she said, "Ahh! Such trouble! The cat ate it."

Nasreddin Hodja looked around and saw the scrawny little cat, looking just as hungry as he felt himself. He grabbed the cat and weighed him. The poor thing weighed exactly two kilograms.

"Well," said the Hodja, "if this is the cat, where is the stew?"

# The Valiant Little Tailor

A little tailor was sitting in his house one summer morning sewing when some flies came buzzing in. The tailor took off his shoe. *SLAM!* Seven flies were squashed underneath — seven! He was so proud he made himself a belt with the words: *7 IN ONE BLOW* stitched upon it. Then he locked up his little house and set off to spread the word of his brave deed around the world.

Another traveller noticed the tailor's belt. 'He must be a mighty warrior,' he thought and hurried to tell the king. The king was delighted and ordered the tailor to be brought before him at once, for he had an important task to give him.

"In the nearest forest there are two giants," the king told the tailor. "They cause all sorts of trouble. If you can get rid of them, I'll give you half of my kingdom and my daughter's hand in marriage!"

So the tailor set out and soon came to the forest. There were the two giants, sleeping under a tree, snoring. The little tailor climbed a tree and threw down a stone onto the chest of one. Immediately the giant woke up and gave his friend a shove. "Stop throwing things!" he roared.

"You must have gone mad," shouted the other giant, "I'm not throwing things at you!"

The tailor waited until the grumbling giants settled

down to sleep again. Then he threw down a bigger stone. The first giant sprang up and punched the second giant on the nose. The second giant hit him straight back — and so it went on, until at last they knocked each other out.

The little tailor hurried back and told the king's men to collect the giants and remove them from the kingdom. "It is done," he told to the king. "Now where is my reward?"

The king kept his promise. And that is how a little tailor married a princess and won half a kingdom — all through swatting flies!

# The Hungry Horse

**A** noble lord wanted to give justice to all his
people, so he placed a bell with a piece of
rope tied to it outside his gate. He promised that
he would help anyone who rang the bell.

One day the bell rang loudly, and when the
lord came out, he was surprised to find a starving
horse there, chewing the end of the rope. One of the
bystanders told how the horse had belonged to a
neighbouring knight. It had carried him safely
through many battles, but now that it was old, its
master had turned it out.

The lord said the horse deserved a
reward for its hard work, and ordered
the knight to give it a place in his
stable and plenty of food for as
long as it lived.

# The Town Mouse and the Country Mouse

**O**nce upon a time, a town mouse went to visit his cousin in the country. The country mouse was poor and lived a simple life. Cheese and bread, and a bed of straw were all he had to offer.

The town mouse wasn't impressed. "Come with me," he said. "I'll show you how to live."

When they arrived at the town mouse's house the town mouse took his cousin into a splendid dining room. There, they found the remains of a fine feast on the table.

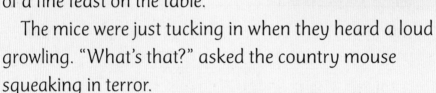

The mice were just tucking in when they heard a loud growling. "What's that?" asked the country mouse squeaking in terror.

"It is only the dogs of the house," answered the town mouse.

"Only the dogs!" gasped the country mouse. "I'm off home to peace and quiet."

# Jorinda and Joringel

There was once an enchanted castle that was home to a witch. If a boy came near it, they would be struck still like a statue, and a girl would be changed into a rare bird. The castle had seven thousand cages of the poor creatures!

One day, a betrothed couple — Jorinda and Joringel — went for a walk and strayed too near the castle. At once Jorinda disappeared and a nightingale appeared in her place, singing sadly. Joringel was frozen as though made of stone. The witch came and caught the bird. After she had left, Joringel found himself able to move again.

That night Joringel dreamt that he found a red flower that had the power to break every evil spell. When he awoke, he set out in search of it, and on the ninth day of looking, he found it. He picked it and walked to the castle.

Carrying the flower, he found he could enter unharmed. He came to a vast room filled with cages. Just as he found his nightingale the witch leapt out at him, but when she was just three paces away she stopped — it was as if she was contained within an invisible box.

Joringel touched the nightingale with the flower and at once Jorinda was standing there. Together they used the flower to turn all the other caged birds back into maidens — and the witch could do nothing but watch.

# How the Rhinoceros got his Skin

**O**nce upon a time, there lived a man who decided to bake a cake. When it was ready, he took it down to the beach to eat, but suddenly a rhinoceros appeared!

Now, in those days the rhinoceros's skin fitted him quite tightly, with no wrinkles. In fact, he could take off his skin – it had three buttons underneath.

The rhino stomped right up to the man and said, "How!"

Of course the man was terribly frightened, so he dropped his cake and climbed straight to the top of a palm tree! The rhinoceros spiked the cake on his horn and ate it. Soon after, the man came down and said:

"*Them that takes cakes*
  *Which the Man bakes*
  *Makes dreadful mistakes.*"

Five weeks later, there was a heatwave, and everybody took off their clothes. The rhinoceros took off his skin and left it on the beach. He waddled into the water to cool down.

Soon after the man came by and saw the skin just lying there. He took that skin, and he shook that skin, and he rubbed that skin full of dry, stale, tickly cake crumbs. Then he climbed up his palm tree and waited.

When the rhinoceros emerged from the water he put on his skin, buttoned it up – and it tickled like cake crumbs in bed! He ran to a palm tree and rubbed and rubbed himself against it. The rhino rubbed so much and so hard that his skin soon became wrinkled all over! He even rubbed the buttons off!

And he went home, very angry and horribly scratchy. Ever since then every rhinoceros has had great folds in his skin and a very bad temper.

# Nasreddin Hodja and the Parrot

One day **Nasreddin Hodja** was walking around the market place when he saw a brightly coloured bird. The price on it was twelve gold coins.

"How can a bird be so expensive?" Hodja asked the shoppers nearby in astonishment.

"It is a special bird," they explained. "It can talk like a human!"

At this Hodja went straight home, grabbed his turkey and brought it to the market place. He stood near the man selling the parrot and yelled, "Turkey for sale! Only ten gold coins!"

"How can a turkey be worth ten gold coins?" the shoppers protested.

"Well, a bird over there is going for twelve," insisted Nasreddin.

"But *that* bird can talk like a human being," the people said.

"Well, *this* bird can THINK like a human being!" replied Nasreddin triumphantly.

# The Two Pots

Two pots had been left on a riverbank. One was made of brass and the other of earthenware. As the tide rose, they both floated downstream. They were tossed this way and that way, and the brass pot cried out, "Don't worry my friend, I will not hit you."

"But I may bash into you by accident," said the earthenware pot. "Whether I hit you, or you hit me, you'll be fine, but I will suffer for it."

# The King o' the Cats

The gravedigger's wife was sitting with her big black cat, Old Tom, when her husband arrived home one evening. "Oh, I have a strange tale to tell you. I was digging away when I saw nine black cats. They were carrying a small coffin covered with black velvet, and at every third step they cried all together, 'Meow —'

"Meow!" said Old Tom.

"Then they all stopped. One came forwards and said to me, 'Tell Tom Tildrum that Tim Toldrum's gone.'"

At this, Old Tom yelled, "What — old Tim is gone! Then I'm the King o' the Cats!" And he rushed up the chimney and was never seen again.

# The Three Billy Goats Gruff

Three billy goats Gruff decided to cross a bridge so they could eat the lush grass in the meadow on the other side of a river. The smallest goat went first, but he was only halfway across when a troll leapt out and roared, "Who's that trit-trotting over my bridge? I'll eat you for dinner."

"Don't eat me," said the goat. "I'm too little. Wait till my big brother comes," and he ran across to safety.

When the second goat tried to cross, the troll once more roared out his threat. But the second goat just said, "Don't eat me, I'm too bony. Wait till my big brother comes," and ran across to safety.

Then the third Billy Goat Gruff stepped onto the bridge. The troll roared out again, "Who's that trit-trotting over my bridge?"

"ME!" said the big Billy Goat Gruff, and he butted the troll right into the river! Then he ran to join his brothers, and they all ate the lush grass.

# The Endless Tale

**M**any years ago in the Far East, there was a great king who loved stories. He said, "The man that can tell me a never-ending story will marry my daughter, and shall be king after me."

The king's daughter was very pretty and many men tried to fulfill the task, but all their stories eventually came to an end. Then one day a stranger from the south came into the palace with a story about locusts.

"A king once stored all his corn in a granary. But a swarm of hungry locusts found a crack that was large enough for one locust to pass through. So one locust went in and carried away a grain of corn, then another locust went in and carried away a grain of corn, then another locust went in and carried away a grain of corn…"

Day after day, week after week, the man said, "Then another locust went in and carried away a grain of corn…"

A month passed, a year passed, and at the end of two years, the king said, "How much longer will the locusts be going in and carrying away corn?"

"Oh King," said the storyteller, "there are many thousands of grains in the granary."

"Man, man," cried the king, "I can listen to it no longer. Take my daughter, be my heir, rule my kingdom. But do not let me hear another word about those horrible locusts!"

# Eat, My Clothes!

**A** peasant boy called Giufà was invited to a wedding, so he put on his only coat, which was very ragged, and set off. The family, when they saw him looking so poor, came near to setting the dogs on him, and offered him no food or drink.

When his mother heard about it, she scrimped and saved and bought him a fine coat, a pair of breeches, and a velvet waistcoat.

At the next wedding he was invited to, Giufà wore his new clothes. This time he was invited to eat with the family. Everyone was very polite to him. Giufà filled his stomach, and then starting putting food into his pockets, coat, and hat saying, "Eat, my clothes, for you are welcome, not I!"

# The Bear and the Fox
# Go into Partnership

The fox called Reynard and the bear called Bruin made up their minds to share a field so that they could grow their own crops. The first year they sowed wheat. "Now we must share and share alike," said Reynard, the fox. "You can have the roots and I will have the tops."

So when they had threshed the crop, the fox got all the grain, while Bruin got nothing but the muddy roots. Bruin didn't like this, but Reynard said it was what they had agreed. "Another year it will be your turn. You can then have the tops, and I will be satisfied with the roots."

Bruin was happy with that. But next spring the crafty Reynard sowed carrots in the field. When autumn came Reynard took the carrots, but Bruin only got the leafy tops.

Bruin realized Reynard had tricked him once more — and the angry bear never spoke to the cunning fox again!

# The Husband of the Rats' Daughter

A rat and his wife had one daughter, the loveliest girl in the rat world. As she grew up, her parents began to look for a suitable husband.

"We should offer her hand in marriage to the sun," said father rat. "There is nothing greater."

So they went to the palace where the sun lived. But when the mother rat told the sun their offer, he replied, "The cloud is greater than me, for he can cover me."

So the mother repeated her proposal to the cloud. "Alas," said the cloud, "the wind is more powerful than me, for he can push me around the sky."

So, turning to the wind, the mother began her little speech once more. "The wall is the proper husband for your daughter," said the wind, "for he has the power to stop me in my flight."

So they gave their offer to the wall, but he declared, "There is someone more powerful than I, and that is the rat. The rat can reduce me to powder, simply with his teeth. If you want a son-in-law who is greater than the whole world, seek him among the rats."

So all three returned home, and the rat's daughter happily married a handsome young rat.

# The Star Money

Long ago, there was a young orphan girl who was so poor that she had nowhere to live. One cold day on her travels, she met a starving beggar. He looked so hungry that she gave him her last piece of bread.

A few miles further on she came across a shivering boy. She took off her jacket and wrapped it around him.

Further on, she saw a beggar girl, stick-thin and wearing rags. The little orphan gave away her own dress to warm her. Next she came to another poor child, whose feet were bare. The girl gave her shoes to the boy.

The orphan girl now had nothing, but she still travelled on. As she walked, she gazed up at the millions of stars in the night sky. They glittered and began to fall – there were coins falling all around her! The girl hurried to gather as many as she could. Soon she had enough to never want for anything ever again – and she lived happily ever after.

# How the Goblins Turned to Stone

Goblins of Holland live deep underground, as daylight turns them to stone. They only come out at night, to cause trouble and mischief. They wear red caps, which make them invisible.

One day, a little Dutch girl called Alida found a goblin cap, and she left a note telling the owner to come to a field that night with all the other goblins to fetch it back. Then she gathered hundreds of men together in the dark. She told them to feel for the goblins, snatch their hats off and then hold them until daylight came. The goblins arrived and the men began to grab, snatch and pull. In a few minutes, hundreds of red caps were in their hands and many wriggling goblins became visible. The men held the goblins firmly and at the first ray of the sun, they all turned to stone. The stones can still be seen in Holland today.

# The Farmer with the Small Barn

A farmer had a barn so small that it only just had room for his cow. His wife begged him to buy a donkey for her to ride. The farmer knew there would not be enough space, but in the end he gave in and bought a donkey.

This made the barn very crowded – the two animals kept jostling each other. In the end, the farmer prayed to God to let the cow escape.

The next morning, the donkey had escaped.

"Dear Lord," the man asked, "with all your wisdom, can't you tell the difference between a donkey and a cow?"

# The Little Mermaid

Once upon a time, a Sea King lived deep under the ocean with his mermaid daughter.

One day the little mermaid was playing at the surface when she saw a ship. In it was a handsome young prince. As she watched, a storm arose and the ship sank!

The little mermaid swam desperately to find the prince and took him to the shore. She was sad, because she knew they couldn't live together. 'I will see if the sea witch can help me,' she thought. She left the prince, and swam to the sea witch's lair.

The sea witch thought for a time, then said, "I can give you legs. And if the prince marries you, you will become human. But if he marries another, you will become foam on the waves."

"I'll do it," said the brave little mermaid.

"But I must be paid," said the witch. "You have the sweetest voice in the ocean. Give it to me."

The little mermaid agreed. The witch took her voice and gave her a potion, and the little mermaid drank it.

When the sun rose, the mermaid found herself lying on the sand. She had legs and feet, and she was wearing clothes! Before her stood the handsome young prince.

The prince asked who she was, but she could not reply. He took her back to his palace and said she could always stay with him.

One morning, the little mermaid woke to the sound of church bells. "Today is my wedding day," the prince explained. "My father has ordered that I get married."

The wedding took place, but the little mermaid was so sad that she decided to leave the party and await her fate on the shore. At the first light of dawn, the little mermaid threw herself into the sea — but she did not become foam. Instead she saw beautiful transparent beings floating all around her. "We are spirits," they said. "We fly around the world doing good deeds. We want you to join us, because you gave up everything for love."

The little mermaid's heart was filled with joy at last, and she flew away with the spirits to be happy forever.

## The Farmers and the Storm

APRIL
14

A group of men were working in a field when a storm broke out. Lightning flashed and thunder crashed. They rushed to a barn but the storm still raged.

"The gods are angry with one of us," the men decided. "Let us put all our hats outside and see which one draws the lightning."

They did so and lightning struck the straw hat of one poor fellow. Seeing this, the others pushed him out into the storm, saying, "Go and receive your punishment."

Not wanting his friends to suffer with him, the man agreed to go. As he stood there trembling, the lightning struck the barn – so only he was left unhurt.

## APRIL 15 The Morning and the Evening Star

**O**nce upon a time there were two stars. One was named Tschen and the other Shen. Both were sons of the Golden King of the Heavens. One day the two stars quarrelled, and made a vow that they would never again look upon each other.

To this day Tschen only appears in the evening, and Shen only appears in the morning, and they are also known as the morning and evening stars.

# Jupiter and the Monkey

Long ago the great god Jupiter, who ruled over the Earth, issued a proclamation to all the beasts. He offered a prize to the one who, in his judgement, produced the most beautiful child.

All the animals were so proud of their children that they were sure they would win the prize. They came in herds and flocks and swarms to make an enormous queue before Jupiter to show him their babies. Among them came the monkey, carrying her baby in her arms. It was a hairless, flat-nosed little thing, and when the gods saw it, they burst into laughter. However, the monkey hugged her baby and said, "I shall always think my baby the most beautiful, for beauty is in the eye of the beholder."

# The Water Nix

**M**any years ago, a brother and sister were playing by a well when the girl toppled in. Her brother reached out to save her, but he fell in too! A mischievous water sprite called a nix lived down below. She grabbed them, saying, "Now you will live with me and do all my work."

The little boy had to chop down trees for firewood and the little girl had to spin at a spinning wheel. They both had to fetch water — in buckets with holes!

After several weeks a chance came for them to escape, so they set off. But the nix ran after them with huge strides. The children knew they could not outrun her.

Quick as a flash, the little girl took her hairbrush from her pocket and threw it behind her. The hairbrush grew and grew — until it was a hill covered in sharp spikes that blocked the water nix's path. The water nix roared with rage, but she slowly picked her way through.

Soon she was gaining on them again, so the little girl threw her pocket mirror behind her as far as she could. The mirror grew and grew — until it was a mountain made entirely of glass. It was so slippery that it was impossible for the nix to cross.

The children found their way back home, and they lived happily ever after.

# Little Tuck

**T**here was once a young boy called Tuck. One day, he had a geography test to revise for, but his mother kept him busy with jobs. He cooked and cleaned, looked after his sister, and even helped an old washerwoman with her washing.

By the time he had finished, dusk was falling and the light was too dim inside the cottage to read – all Tuck could do was go to bed. He put his geography book under his pillow, because he had heard one of his friends say that information could sink into your brain while you slept.

Tuck didn't realize that the old lady he'd helped knew magic. She rewarded his kindness by sending him a vivid dream, in which he met animals from all over the world. They told him all about their countries and the names of the capital cities so that when Tuck awoke the following morning, he knew everything that came up in his test!

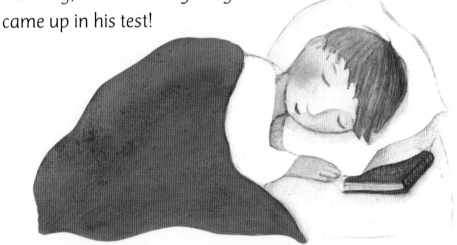

# The Wolf and the Shepherd

A shepherd was out on a hillside one day when he found a tiny lost wolf cub. He decided to take the cub home and rear it with his dogs.

The cub grew up, and learnt to herd the sheep. If ever a wolf stole a sheep from the flock, the tame wolf would join the dogs in hunting it down. But if the dogs failed to find the thief, the tame wolf would continue on alone. When it found the culprit, it would share in the feast. And if some time passed without a sheep being carried off by a wolf, the tame wolf would steal one for itself.

Eventually, the shepherd became suspicious. He kept a close watch on the tame wolf, and one day he caught it in the act of stealing a sheep. The shepherd was sad, but he ordered his dogs to chase away the wolf — for it was never truly tame.

# Momotaro

**O**ne day, a woman who had no children found a baby boy in a peach. She brought him up as her own and called him Momotaro, which means 'son of a peach'.

When Momotaro was seventeen he set out to steal an ogre's fortune. He had not gone far when he met a wasp.

"Give me a share of your food," said the wasp, "and I will help you."

"Yes of course," said Momotaro.

Next he met a crab, and the same agreement was made. The same happened with a chestnut and a millstone.

When they reached the ogre's house. The chestnut hid in the ash of the fire, the crab hid in the washing pan, the wasp hid in a dark corner, the millstone climbed onto the roof, and Momotaro hid in the garden.

Before long the ogre appeared, and went to the fire to warm himself. The chestnut threw cinders over the ogre's hands. The ogre ran to the washing pan but the crab pinched his fingers. Snatching his hands out of the pan, the ogre leapt into the corner where the wasp stung him. The ogre tried to run out of the room, but down came the millstone with a crash on his head and knocked him out.

So, with the help of the friends he had made through his kindness, Momotaro got all the ogre's gold and his fortune was made.

# The Stone Soup

**M**any years ago, three poor soldiers walked into a village, begging for food. The villagers told them sadly that no one had anything to spare. So the first soldier said, "Very well. We will teach you how to make soup from stones."

They put a pot on a fire and dropped in three stones. "This will be a fine soup," the second soldier said, "but a pinch of salt and some parsley would make it wonderful!"

Up jumped a villager, and returned with parsley, salt and also a turnip.

Soon other villagers were donating barley, carrots, beef and cream and everyone was sitting down to eat the delicious soup. They thanked the soldiers for teaching them their secret. The third soldier turned to the crowd, and said, "There is no secret — it is only by sharing that we may make a feast."

# The Father and his Daughters

**A** **man once had two daughters,** one of whom grew up to marry a gardener, while the other daughter married a potter.

After a time, the man went to visit his daughters. First, he went to the gardener's wife. He asked her how things were going. She replied, "I wish we could have some heavy rain. All our fruit and vegetables are about to wither and die."

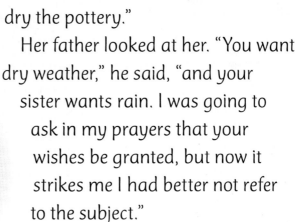

Then the man went to the potter's wife. She said, "I wish we could have some dry weather, to dry the pottery."

Her father looked at her. "You want dry weather," he said, "and your sister wants rain. I was going to ask in my prayers that your wishes be granted, but now it strikes me I had better not refer to the subject."

# The Buckwheat

Long ago, there was a field of buckwheat. The buckwheat did not bend in the wind like other grains, instead, they stood straight and stiff, holding their heads up proudly.

One night, a terrible storm came and all the plants in the cornfields folded their leaves and bowed their heads to avoid harm. But the buckwheat stood up straighter than ever.

"Bow down," urged the old willow tree.

"Nothing can make us bow down," said the buckwheat. And boldly the buckwheat looked straight up, while lightning blazed across the sky.

When the storm had died away, the wildflowers raised their heads. They felt quite refreshed by the rain. However, the buckwheat was a sorry sight. They were scorched black by the lightning and lay across the earth, defeated after all.

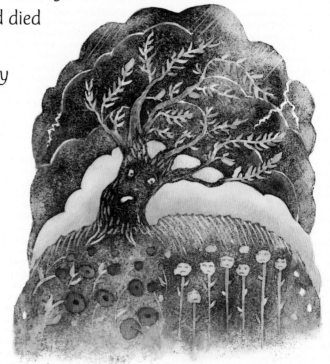

# The Shipwrecked Man and the Sea

**A** **man who had been shipwrecked** was struggling in the
water. He was about to give up when finally he was
washed up on a beach, and at once fell into a deep sleep.

When the man awoke, he was furious, and he raged at
the sea, which was now completely smooth. "How deceitful
you are!" he cried. "You draw people in by showing your
peaceful side, but when you have us in your power, you
become cruel and punish us."

To his huge surprise, the sea then
appeared in the form of a woman, and
replied, "Don't blame me, O sailor, it's
the fault of the winds. By nature I am
calm and safe, but the winds buffet
me with their gusts and gales, and
whip me into a monster."

# The Troll who
# Wrote a Letter

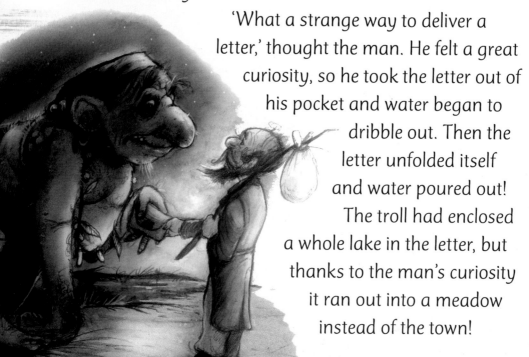

A troll had just built his house on a riverbank when the people of the town built a church next to it. The troll decided to leave, but he was angry with the people for forcing him out of his old home.

Not long after, the troll met a man on his way to the town. The troll had been waiting for a chance like this. "Will you be so kind as to take a letter to the town?"

The man said he would gladly do so. The troll took a letter out of his pocket and said, "Please throw this letter over the churchyard wall."

'What a strange way to deliver a letter,' thought the man. He felt a great curiosity, so he took the letter out of his pocket and water began to dribble out. Then the letter unfolded itself and water poured out! The troll had enclosed a whole lake in the letter, but thanks to the man's curiosity it ran out into a meadow instead of the town!

# Nasreddin Hodja and the Naughty Boy

One day Nasreddin Hodja bought a donkey. He started to walk home, leading it behind him, when two boys decided to trick him.

One of them snuck up behind Nasreddin, loosened the donkey's halter and put it over his own head. The other boy took the donkey away to sell.

When they reached home, Nasreddin Hodja saw the boy.

"Who are you?" he said.

"I misbehaved and made my mother miserable. She put a curse on me and I turned into a donkey. When you bought me, the curse ended."

"I will let you go, but never again torment your mother," said Nasreddin.

The next day Nasreddin went looking for a donkey to buy. He saw the donkey he'd bought the day before. He went up to it and whispered, "You naughty boy! You disobeyed your mother again, didn't you?"

# Foolish Hans Saves a Man

**A** man had climbed a tree to pick some apples and couldn't get down again.

"Help me!" he called out to some passersby. Foolish Hans happened to be among them and announced that he would save the man. He took a long rope and threw it up to the man in the tree, telling him to tie it around his waist. "How will this help?" the people asked.

"Trust me," Hans said, "I saved a man like this once before."

The man did as he was told, Hans gave a strong tug and pulled the man out of the tree. He fell to the ground with a bump and was quite hurt.

Hans scratched his head thoughtfully, "Now I come to think of it," he said, "the last man I saved was in a river."

# The Ogre's Bride

**M**olly **was about to be married** to an ogre. Her father had promised the match, but as she didn't want the ogre for a husband she decided to find a way out of it.

When the ogre came to her father's house to talk about the wedding she cooked a fine stew. "What a delicious meal!" said the ogre.

"Made with dead rats!" lied Molly.

'How I will save money when I marry her,' thought the ogre. "When can we marry?" he asked.

"Only once you've built me a 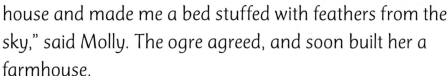 house and made me a bed stuffed with feathers from the sky," said Molly. The ogre agreed, and soon built her a farmhouse.

The very day it was complete there was a snowstorm, and Molly sent for the ogre. "Now you see the feathers falling," she said, pointing at the snow, "use them to fill the bed."

The ogre carried in shovelfuls of snow but it melted as fast as he put it in. Towards night the room got so cold that the snow stopped melting and the bed was soon filled. Molly came to inspect the ogre's work, and said, "Very good. Rest here tonight. Tomorrow we will be married."

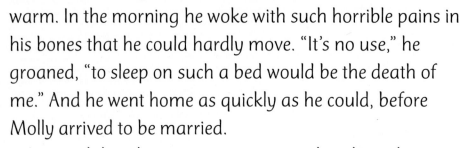

So the tired ogre lay down on the bed he had filled with snow, but he could not get warm. In the morning he woke with such horrible pains in his bones that he could hardly move. "It's no use," he groaned, "to sleep on such a bed would be the death of me." And he went home as quickly as he could, before Molly arrived to be married.

It is said that the ogre never recovered and was less powerful than before. As for Molly, with a new fine farmhouse she had many offers of marriage, and lived happily ever after.

# The Donkey, the Fox and the Lion

There was once a donkey and a fox who set out to look for something to eat, but they hadn't gone far when they saw a lion coming their way. The donkey looked around for a place to hide, while the fox thought he saw a way of saving himself.

He approached the lion and whispered, "If you let me go, I will help you get the donkey." The lion agreed. The fox then returned to the donkey and told him that he had found a hiding place. Then he led the donkey over a pit that a hunter had dug as a trap, and the donkey fell straight down into it.

But once the donkey was caught, the first thing the lion did was pounce on the fox and gobble him up. Then he had plenty of time to eat the donkey.

# The Fawn and his Mother

**A** **female deer** had a baby fawn, which she cared for very well. The fawn grew to be big and strong. However he seemed to be afraid of everything he came across, and jumped at the slightest thing.

One day, the mother deer said, "My boy, nature has given you a powerful body and a stout pair of antlers. You could charge at anything with those and run them right through! Why do you run away from everything?"

Just then they both heard the sound of a pack of hounds — they knew that huntsmen must be coming. And with that, they both ran off as fast as their legs could carry them. 'Sometimes running away is the right option,' thought the mother deer.

# The Cunning Rat

A rat was about to come out of a hole when he noticed a cat waiting just outside. So the mouse went back inside and asked a friend to join him on his walk.

"Very well," said the friend, "I will go with you. Lead on."

"No, indeed — after you, sir," exclaimed the other.

Pleased with this politeness, the friend went ahead, and leaving the hole first, immediately had to run for his life as the cat made a pounce at him. The other rat scampered out safely after!

# The Iron Stove

A princess was once walking in a forest when she found an iron stove. Out of the stove came a voice crying, "Help me! I am an enchanted prince. I beg you to free me. If you can help, I shall make you my queen!"

"I will," promised the princess.

She took a knife from her bag and scraped a hole in the stove until it was large enough for the prince to climb out.

"I thank you with all my heart," the prince said. Then he asked the princess to marry him and travel to his kingdom — and she said yes! First though, she wanted to say goodbye to her father.

"Very well," agreed the prince, "but you mustn't speak more than three words. I will wait here for you."

Of course, the princess forgot her promise and spoke more than three words to her father. At once a magic wind wiped all memories of her from the prince's head, and carried him back to his own kingdom.

The princess began a long search to find her prince. Late one night, she came across a tiny cottage. It was the home of a toad. The princess begged him to help her, and he gave her a map and a magic nut.

The princess followed the map, though the way was difficult and dangerous — she had to climb a glass mountain, and cross a field with plants as sharp as swords, and swim across a lake as wide as the sea.

When at last the princess reached her sweetheart's castle, her clothes were so ragged and tattered that she wasn't allowed in. Then she remembered the nut and cracked it open. Inside was a beautiful gown. She put it on at once.

As soon as the prince saw her, he remembered her. The two were married and lived happily ever after.

# The Fierce Lion and the Cunning Little Jackal

In the jungle there lived a great lion. He killed and ate all the other animals until one day there were only a few left. The little jackal was scared he would be next, so he made a plan.

He went to the lion's den and said to the lion, "I'm so frightened! There is another lion in the jungle who is even fiercer than you."

"What!" roared the lion. "Lead me to him."

So the little jackal led the lion to a deep well. Then pointing down to the lion's own reflection in the water, the jackal said, "He's down there!"

At once the lion jumped in to kill his deadly foe, but nothing was there — only his reflection.

Try as he might, the lion could not climb out of the well — he may still be there now. And the clever little jackal is safe.

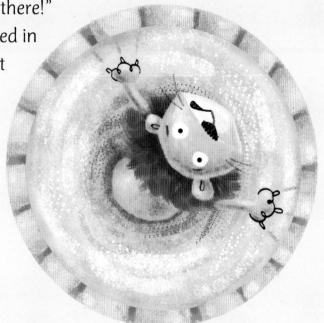

# The Swan and the Goose

There was a rich man who bought a goose and a swan. He fed the goose well, planning to cook it for a feast one day. He enjoyed listening to the swan's beautiful song, however, so he decided to keep it as a pet.

The time finally arrived for the man to hold his feast. His cook made many delicious dishes, then went to catch the goose for cooking. But it was so dark outside that the cook could hardly tell one bird from another and by mistake he caught the swan instead of the goose. The swan, thinking it was about to be killed, burst into one last beautiful song. Of course then the cook realized that he had the wrong bird – and so the swan was saved by its singing.

# The Twelve Huntsmen

**A** **prince and princess** were once deeply in love, but the prince's dying father had arranged for his son to marry someone else — and the wedding was to take place that week. When the princess heard this, she hatched a plan.

First she asked her father to send his servants to find eleven girls that looked just like her, and this was done. Then the princess asked for twelve suits of huntsmen's clothes to be made, and twelve fine horses to be brought, and this was also done.

The princess and the eleven girls put on the clothes, and set off on horseback to her sweetheart's castle, where he was now king. When the twelve fine huntsman arrived at the castle the king hired them at once — he did not recognize his love among them.

The next day, the king went hunting with his fine new companions. As they were riding, a messenger arrived with news that the king's bride-to-be would be arriving at the castle that day.

When the princess heard this, she fell from her horse in a faint.

The king raced to her side, thinking that the brave
captain of his huntsmen was ill. As he leant over, carefully
removing the captain's hat and gloves, the king seemed to
wake from the sadness that had sickened him since he had
given up his love. And when he recognized his ring on the
captain's finger, he knew it was his princess in disguise and
he gasped with joy. "Forgive me, father," he murmured,
"but I cannot marry any other."

The two sent a messenger to explain to the other
princess that the new king was very sorry, but could not
marry her. As luck would have it, she wasn't disappointed
— she had fallen in love with the king's friend, a duke. And
so two weddings
were celebrated
— everyone
was very
happy indeed.

# The Butterfly

There was once a butterfly who wanted to fall in love. He didn't want a butterfly for a wife though — he wanted to marry a flower. The problem was, he couldn't decide which was the prettiest.

He flew to the violets, but he thought their scent was too strong.

He flew to the tulips, but their colours were too bright. One day while still in search of the perfect bloom, the butterfly flew in through a window. The people in the room caught him and pinned him to a piece of cardboard. "Now I'm sitting on a stalk, just like the flowers," the butterfly sighed. "And it isn't fun."

Too late, he realized he had been mistaken all along. "Beauty alone isn't enough to make you happy," he sighed. "To be happy, you must have freedom and sunshine."

# The Mice and the Weasels

The mice and the weasels fought many battles, and the mice always lost.

At a meeting to discuss tactics, one old mouse said, "We need generals to direct our troops."

This made a lot of sense to the other mice and they at once chose the biggest among them to be their generals.

The generals put on large helmets decorated with plumes of straw and led the mice into battle. But they were defeated again and sent scampering back to their holes.

However, this time the generals had great difficulty squeezing into their holes because their helmets were so big. The mice learnt a hard lesson that day — greatness carries its own dangers.

# The Husband who was to Mind the House

**O**nce upon a time there was a man who thought his
wife never did anything right in the house. "Well," said
his wife, "tomorrow let's change jobs. I'll go out to the
fields, and you can mind the house."

So the next morning the wife went out with the scythe,
and the man began to do the work at home. First of all he
wanted to churn butter to make cream, but when he had
churned for a while, he got thirsty, and went down to the
cellar to tap a barrel of ale. He had just started when he
heard a commotion in the kitchen above.
When he got there he found
the pig rolling in the cream
on the floor. By the time he
had put the pig out and
returned to the cellar, all the ale
had run out of the barrel.

The man was mopping the cellar floor when he
remembered that the cow hadn't eaten. He decided it was
too far to take the cow to the meadow, so he pulled her
onto the roof, for it was an earth roof with a fine crop of
grass. Worried that the cow might fall off the roof, he tied
one end of a rope to the cow's leg and slipped the other end

down the chimney and tied it around his own leg.

The man was feeling very pleased with himself when the cow fell off the roof, dragging the man up the chimney! There he was stuck, with the cow hanging halfway down the wall outside.

When his wife got home and saw the cow hanging there, she cut the rope with her scythe. As she did this, her husband fell into the porridge pot and he never said a word against her again.

# Nasreddin Hodja Rescues the Moon

One evening Nasreddin Hodja went to fetch some water. Looking into the well he saw the moon's reflection. Thinking the moon had fallen in, he took a rope with a hook at one end and lowered it down.

The hook caught on a rock, so when Hodja pulled, it broke and he fell onto his back. As he gazed at the sky he sighed with relief. "I am hurt," he said, "but at least the moon is back in the sky!"

# The Trumpeter Taken Prisoner

**O**nce there was a brave army trumpeter who strayed too close to the enemy and was captured. The young trumpeter begged for mercy.

"Look at me – I am not a fighter," he said. "I don't even carry a weapon. All I do is blow this trumpet – and how can that hurt you? So please spare my life, I have done nothing to you."

But the enemy soldiers answered grimly, "By sounding out the orders, you guide and encourage your soldiers in battle. They and you have killed hundreds of our men, so now you must pay the price for your music."

# The Sorcerer's Apprentice

**A** **sorcerer left his workshop** to visit a friend, leaving his young apprentice with water to carry and cleaning to do. After a while, the apprentice grew bored of the hard work and looked into the sorcerer's magic book to try and find a spell to help him. He enchanted a broom to sweep and carry water, and for a while it worked. But the broom brought bucket after bucket of water until the floor was awash.

The apprentice then realized he didn't know how to stop the spell! He seized an axe and cut the broom in half, but that made two brooms that worked even faster. Soon there was so much water that the apprentice was nearly swimming! Just in time, the old sorcerer came back and broke the spell. And luckily for the apprentice he forgave his pupil for interfering.

# The Fool in India

**A** foolish man was once travelling from one village to another, but lost his way. When he asked for help, the people said to him, "When you get to the riverbank, take the path that goes up by the tree."

The fool reached the river and thinking that he was following their instructions, climbed up a great tree. The bough bent and he nearly fell into the river.

While he was clinging to it, there came along an elephant and its driver. The fool called to the driver, saying, "Please, help! I can't get down."

The elephant-driver took hold of the fool's feet with both his hands, but his elephant carried on walking! The driver found himself clinging to the feet of the fool, who was clinging to the end of the tree.

Then the fool said to the driver, "Sing something loudly, so that the people hear us, and come and help."

But the elephant-driver sang so sweetly that the fool let go of the tree so he could applaud. Immediately he and the driver fell into the river with a splash!

# The Hare and the Tortoise

**A** **hare was once boasting** to the other animals about how speedy he was. To prove it he asked the tortoise to race him.

"Ready, set, go!" bellowed the ox.

The hare darted out of sight. As he rounded the first bend, he decided to have a laugh at the tortoise's expense. He lay down under a tree and pretended to nap — just to show that he could stop to sleep and still win. But it was so lovely and cool that the hare really did fall asleep!

Slowly, slowly, the tortoise plodded on… past the sleeping hare… until the finish line was in sight.

The hare woke with a start and bounded after the tortoise — but it was too late! The tortoise crossed the finish line before he could catch up. "Slow and steady wins the race," said the tortoise.

# The Money Pig

**I**n the playroom, lots of toys were lying about. There were teddy bears and building blocks, drawing pencils and toy soldiers, a dolls' house and a train set. High up on top of a cupboard was a china money box, in the shape of a pig. It was stuffed full of coins.

The money pig was proud of itself. It knew that what it held would have bought all the other toys — and they knew it too.

One night, one of the dolls suggested excitedly, "Shall we stage our own play?"

All the toys jumped up and down in excitement shouting, "Yes! Yes! Let's!"

"I haven't decided if I will join in," the money pig sniffed. "But one thing's for sure — I shall stay up here in my high position and you will have to involve me in the game like that."

"Very well," said the toys, eager to begin.

Thoughtfully, they pushed and dragged the toy theatre in front of the cupboard so the money pig could see directly in. Then they all took turns on the stage, acting out different people having afternoon tea together.

In fact, it would have been better for the pig if he had joined in with the play because all of a sudden, someone bumped into the cupboard. The money pig toppled off and smashed to pieces. Next day, the family swept up all the broken bits and put them in the bin. By afternoon, a new money pig was standing on top of the cupboard – its tummy empty.

# The Frog and the Snail

A frog entered into a bet with a snail as to which of them would be the first to reach the city. The frog, of course, believed that he would win because he could travel so much faster than the snail.

As they started out the frog made fun of the snail: "Don't crawl along so. Instead hop like I do, otherwise you'll never win." Then away he hopped.

However, arriving at the city, he found that the city gate was closed, so he had to wait until morning when the gate would be opened.

In the meantime the snail crawled steadily onward, and she too finally arrived at the city. Of course, she also found the gate closed, but for her that was no problem. She simply crawled up and over it, and thus won the bet.

# The Four Oxen and the Lion

**O**nce upon a time there were four oxen who lived in a field. A lion regularly used to prowl around, looking for a chance to catch one for dinner. He tried many times, but whenever he came near, they all stood with their tails together. In this way, the lion was met by the horns of one of the oxen from whichever direction he approached — and very long, sharp horns they were too.

One day, however, the oxen argued among themselves, and each stomped off to a different corner of the field to graze. The lion was delighted — now the oxen would be much easier to catch. For united we stand, divided we fall.

# The Lion, the Goat and the Baboon

**The lion and the goat** were once happily married and had lots of little baby goats.

One day, when the goat went to market, a baboon knocked on the door. The polite lion invited him into his house to meet his children.

The baboon looked at the little goats and said, "Why, they look very tasty, you know."

The lion didn't know what to do. The little goats ran and hid, for the baboon was much bigger than them, with long sharp teeth.

Mother goat arrived home soon after, and the lion quietly warned her of their guest's words. She thought for a minute then fetched some treacle. The lion tasted it, and said, "It's very good, what is it?"

The goat answered loudly, "It's baboon's blood."

At this the baboon rushed off and never came near them again.

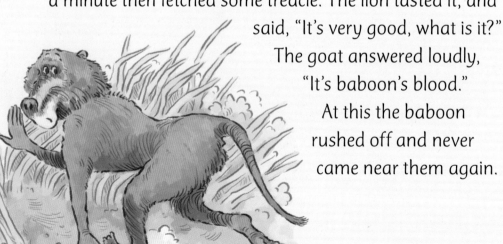

# The Two Travellers and the Farmer

A traveller came upon a farmer working in a field. "What sort of people live in the next town?" the traveller asked.

"What were the people like where you're from?" replied the farmer.

"Selfish, lazy, stupid, and not one of them to be trusted. I'm happy to be leaving."

"Is that so?" replied the farmer. "Well, I'm afraid that you'll find the same sort in the next town."

Sometime later another stranger, coming from the same direction stopped to talk to the farmer. "What sort of people live in the next town?" he asked.

"What were the people like where you've come from?" replied the farmer once again.

"The best people in the world. Hardworking, honest, and friendly. I'm sorry to be leaving them."

"Don't worry," said the farmer. "You'll find the same sort in the next town."

# The Frog Prince

Long ago, there lived a king who had three daughters. Everyone agreed that the youngest princess was loveliest of all.

One hot day, the youngest princess lost her golden ball in a well. She sank down onto the mossy ground and started to cry.

"Don't cry," said a croaky voice. "I can get your ball back."

The princess looked up, startled. "Just promise," said the frog, "that we will be best friends. I want to eat off your golden plates and sleep in your bed."

"Yes, yes," agreed the princess hurriedly.

The frog jumped into the well and reappeared holding the golden ball. The princess was delighted but forgot all about her promise and ran off. That evening, at the palace there was a knocking at the door and a voice croaked, "Let me in!"

The princess grew pale. She told her father what had happened. The king looked grave. "You made a promise and you must keep it," he said firmly.

So the youngest princess let the frog in.

"Lift me up so I can sit and eat with you off your golden plates," the frog croaked.

When the frog's tummy was full, he gave a yawn.

"Delicious," he said. "Now let's sleep."

The princess carried him upstairs to her bedroom. She threw back the quilt and tucked the frog into the bed. Then something very strange happened. The frog transformed into a handsome prince. The prince explained how a wicked witch had enchanted him. The princess was the only one who could save him and, by carrying out her promise, she had broken the spell.

The prince and princess fell in love, and it wasn't long before they set off to the prince's kingdom in a golden carriage drawn by eight white horses. There they married and lived happily ever after.

# Look Where You Lost It

**O**ne summer evening, the front garden of the coffee house was well lit by the gas lamps placed on the few wooden tables. Nasreddin Hodja was, however, troubled. He was searching for something on the ground.

"What are you looking for?" some people nearby asked.

"I lost a gold coin in that alley," he said.

The other customers were mystified, "Then why are you looking for it here? You should search the alley!"

Nasreddin Hodja answered simply, "But it is dark over there and I can't see anything. Here it is nice and bright, so I will search here, where I can see better."

# The Farmer and Fortune

**A** farmer was digging in his field one morning, when to his amazement he dug up a pot of golden coins. He was overjoyed at his discovery. From then on, every day he went to pray at the shrine of the Goddess of the Earth to say thank you for his find. However, the Goddess of Fortune came to hear about this and was jealous.

She came to see the farmer and angrily demanded, "Why do you give the Goddess of the Earth the credit for the gift that I gave you? You have not once thought of thanking me for your good luck! However, should you be unlucky enough to lose what you have gained, I know very well that you would blame me, Fortune, for your bad luck."

# The Goose-girl

Long ago a queen had a beautiful daughter who was going to be married to a prince from a nearby kingdom. The queen gave the princess a talking horse named Falada to ride on the journey to the prince's castle, and the princess set off with her waiting-maid.

However, when they stopped for the princess to drink from a stream, the waiting-maid forced the princess to swap clothes with her. Then the wicked maid climbed onto Falada's back and they continued their journey.

When they arrived at the prince's kingdom, the king and prince greeted them. Of course, they took the wicked maid to be the princess, and led her into the palace, leaving the true princess outside. The king said she could help Conrad, a servant, look after the geese.

The next morning the wicked maid ordered that Falada be sent away so he couldn't reveal what she had done. Conrad and the true princess passed by with the geese just as Falada was being turned away from the castle.

"Oh Falada, must you go?" the princess asked Falada.

And Falada replied, "I must, Princess. If she knew this, your mother's heart would break."

Conrad heard these strange words and decided he would tell the king that evening.

As they neared the water meadows, the princess let

down her long golden hair. Conrad thought it was beautiful, and went to touch it. But the princess called out, "Blow, blow, the gentle wind, I say; Blow Conrad's little hat away; Make him chase it here and there, Until once more I've braided my hair." And such a strong gust of wind blew that Conrad had to chase his hat across the meadow.

That evening Conrad told the king what he had heard and seen. The king then questioned the princess, but she was too frightened to tell him the truth. At last the king sighed, "If you will not tell your troubles to me, tell them to this iron stove."

But the king listened at the door, so he overheard when she said, "Here am I, doomed to be a goose-girl, while the false waiting-maid steals my bridegroom."

The next day the king ordered that the goose-girl be dressed in royal robes. The wicked maid was banished from the kingdom, and the princess was married to the prince. They lived happily ever after.

# The Jackdaw and the Eagle

A young jackdaw once saw a majestic eagle launch himself from a rock to seize a lamb and carry it off.

The jackdaw was full of admiration and decided to try the same thing. He dived upon a large ram but his claws became entangled in its fleece and he was not able to get himself free.

The shepherd laughed when he saw what had happened. Once he had cut the jackdaw free, he took him home and gave him to his children.

The children asked, "What sort of a bird is it?"

The shepherd replied, "It is a jackdaw, but it would like you to think it is an eagle."

# The Twelve Dancing Princesses

**O**nce upon a time, there was a king who had twelve
beautiful daughters. He could not understand one
thing about them though – every morning, their shoes
were worn through. The king announced that if anyone
could discover what was going on, they could marry
whichever princess they liked best. Many young men came
to try their luck, but each time they fell asleep before
finding out.

Then one day a soldier arrived in the kingdom and
decided to find out what the princesses did each night. He
took the advice of a wise old woman who told him not to
drink anything the princesses gave him. She also gave him
a cloak, and said, "When you wear this, you will be
invisible."

The soldier set off for the castle. In the evening, he was
shown into the princesses' bedroom and the king locked
the door. One princess brought the soldier a goblet of wine
but he didn't drink it. He then got into bed and pretended
to sleep.

The twelve princesses then put on their finest dresses
and climbed down through a trapdoor underneath one
of the beds. Quickly, the soldier put on the magic cloak and
followed them.

He came out into daylight. The princesses were travelling

in boats to an island. There was one boat left, and the
soldier jumped in and followed the girls to a castle. Inside,
the great hall was decorated for a magnificent ball with
glittering, golden trees. The soldier reached up to break off
a twig to take back as proof.

The princesses joined the ball, and danced and danced
for hours. When their shoes were quite worn out, they
started back for home. The soldier raced ahead of them
and lay back down on the bed, so they found him as they
had left him – seemingly asleep.

The next morning he went to the king and told the tale
of the trapdoor and the island, and how the princesses had
danced all night. To prove it, he showed the king the
golden twig. The king called for the princesses, who
admitted the truth at once. The king told the soldier he
could choose a princess to be his wife. He chose the
youngest princess and after they were married, he danced
with her every day.

# The Beetle

**The emperor's horse** was a magnificent animal, with intelligent eyes and a mane like silk. The emperor thought his brave horse should have the best of everything, so he ordered the royal blacksmith to make him horseshoes of pure gold.

A tiny beetle living in the stable thought he should have gold shoes made for his feet too. "I live in the royal stable too," said the beetle, "So I also belong to the emperor!"

But the blacksmith only laughed at him.

The beetle sulked for a while, and then a thought struck him. He flew up and sat proudly on the horse's head.

"Now I'm the horse's rider," he cried, "and it's quite clear to me the horse was given golden shoes because of me. That's what I deserve — a horse with golden shoes!"

# The Donkey and the Wolf

A donkey was once grazing in a meadow when he caught sight of his enemy, the wolf, approaching. He knew he would be eaten unless he came up with a plan. So when the wolf reached him, the donkey said cunningly, "I have a thorn in my foot. Please would you pull it out? Otherwise, when you eat me, it might hurt you."

"How thoughtful of you," growled the wolf. He told the donkey to lift up his foot, and set his mind to getting out the thorn. But the donkey suddenly kicked out with his heels, hitting the wolf hard. Then he galloped away as fast as he could.

Sore and rather dazed, the wolf growled to himself, "It serves me right – I should have stuck to what I'm good at."

# The Pointless Feast

One day a fox passed a lovely vineyard surrounded by a tall fence with a small hole in it. The fox could see what luscious grapes grew inside the vineyard, but the hole was too small for him to fit through. He ate nothing for three days until he became so thin that he managed to squeeze through.

Inside the vineyard the fox began to eat. He grew bigger and fatter than ever before. Then he wanted to get out of the vineyard, but now the hole was too small again. So, as before, he ate nothing for three days, and just about managed to slip through the hole again.

Turning his head towards the vineyard, the poor fox said, "How pointless it was to eat that delicious fruit. I'm as thin as when I came in."

# The Snail and the Rose Tree

**O**nce upon a time, there was a garden where a beautiful rose tree bloomed. Under it sat a snail. "Just wait," he muttered. "One day I'll do better things than grow roses."

"How exciting!" replied the rose tree. "I can't wait to see what you will do."

"Well," remarked the snail. "Have you ever thought about why you bloom?"

"No," said the rose tree. "I bloom because I feel so glad about everything."

Then a memory struck her. "I remember a little girl picking one rose and giving it to her mother. It made me so happy that I wished to make many more."

"Hmmph!" said the snail, creeping back into his shell and closing up the entrance.

Years rolled by and the snail crumbled into the earth – and the rose tree too. But other rose trees bloomed, bringing happiness to many people. And other snails crept into their houses, closed up the entrances, and refused to see the beauty of the world.

# Teeny-tiny

**O**nce upon a time there was a teeny-tiny old woman. She lived in a teeny-tiny house in a teeny-tiny street with a teeny-tiny cat. One day the teeny-tiny woman went for a teeny-tiny walk. She saw a teeny-tiny bone lying on top of a teeny-tiny grave. She put the teeny-tiny bone in her teeny-tiny pocket and went home to her teeny-tiny house. She sat in her teeny-tiny chair and heard a teeny-tiny voice say, "Where is my teeny-tiny bone?"

The teeny-tiny woman sat up in her teeny-tiny chair and said in her teeny-tiny voice, "TAKE IT!"

And a teeny-tiny ghost ran out of the teeny-tiny house, down the teeny-tiny street into the teeny-tiny graveyard — with the teeny-tiny bone in its teeny-tiny hand!

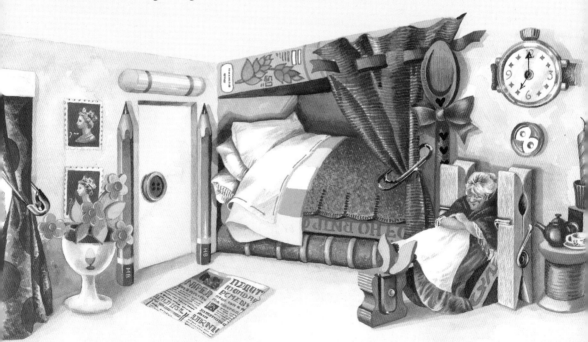

# How the Dragon was Tricked

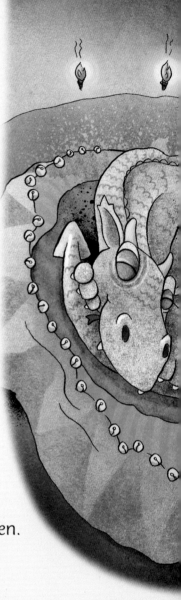

A young man once went to the king and asked to marry his daughter. The king said, "Bring me the covering from the bed of the great dragon, and I will think about it."

So the young man went away to the dragon's house and climbed up onto the roof. Then he let himself down through a window in the ceiling on a rope, and tried to hook the bed covering to draw it up. But the dragon woke, pulled the young man into the room and tied him up!

The following morning the dragoness took hold of the young man, but as she untied the cords, he pushed her into the oven. Then he snatched up the bed covering and carried it to the king.

"That is not enough," said the king. "Bring me the dragon himself."

"It shall be done," answered the youth. So he disguised himself as a beggar and went again to the dragon's house. The young man found the dragon making a box. "What is

the box for?" he asked.

"It is for the man who pushed my wife into the oven and stole my bed covering," said the dragon.

"He deserves nothing better," answered the beggar. "Still, that box doesn't look big enough."

"You are wrong," said the dragon tucking himself inside the box. "The box is large enough even for me."

Quick as a flash, the young man clapped the lid on tight, and drove in nails to make it tighter still. Then he took the box on his back and brought it to the king — who finally let him marry his daughter.

# The Nurse and the Wolf

A nurse was once looking after a child who kept crying. "Be quiet now," she said, "or I'll give you to the wolf."

A wolf was passing under the window and heard the nurse say this. So he sat down and waited.

'The child is sure to cry again soon,' he thought, 'then the nurse will give it to me.'

When the child cried again the wolf sat up under the window and looked at the nurse, wagging his tail. But all the nurse did was gasp in horror and slam the window shut. She let out a shriek and the dogs of the house came bounding out, snarling.

The wolf realized that the nurse hadn't meant what she said, and he fled.

# Androcles and the Lion

**T**here was once a slave named Androcles who managed
to escape his master, and flee into the forest. There he
discovered a lion groaning with
pain. Androcles saw the lion's
paw had a huge thorn
stuck in it. He pulled out
the thorn and the lion
bowed its head to
Androcles
and licked
his hand.

A few days later,
Androcles was recaptured and condemned to fight with
beasts in the Roman arena. He was led out and stood in
terror as a lion was released and came bounding towards
him. Suddenly the lion looked at Androcles and stopped.
Then it licked his hands. It was the lion from the forest!

Everyone was amazed, and the emperor summoned
Androcles, who told his story. The emperor pardoned
Androcles and let him and the lion go free.

# The Traveller and the Farmer

A traveller came upon a farmer one afternoon and called out: "How long will it take me to get to the next town?"

"I can't really say," replied the farmer. The traveller strode away.

"About an hour," shouted the farmer after him.

"Why didn't you say so when I first asked?"

"Because I didn't know how fast you were walking then."

# The Fisherman and his Wife

Once upon a time, there was a poor fisherman who lived in a shack by the sea. One day, he caught a fish, which to his surprise, spoke to him and begged to be allowed to return to the water.

The fisherman did as the fish asked, but when he told his wife, she was angry. "You should have asked for a wish!" she said. "I want to live in a castle. Go and wish for one."

The man went and called the fish and asked for his wish. And the fish said, "Go home. It is already done."

So the man went home and instead of the shack he found a stone castle. "Isn't it beautiful! Look at it all!" said his wife. And they enjoyed a feast and went to bed, happy with their grand new home.

The next morning the wife prodded her husband awake and said, "Get up. I want to be queen! Go and ask the fish to grant me this wish." So the fisherman went and asked the fish, which said, "Go home. She is queen already."

When the fisherman came to where the castle had been he saw instead a gleaming palace. His wife was sitting on a huge silver throne, wearing a golden crown on her head.

The next morning, the fisherman's wife announced, "Husband, I know I am now the queen but I want to be able to order the moon to rise and the sun to set – I want to be God."

Now the fisherman was afraid, but he had to go and ask the fish. The fish rose from the crashing waves and said, "What can your wife want now?"

"Alas," whispered the fisherman, quaking, "she wants to be God."

"Go," said the fish, "you will find her back in the shack."

And there they are both living there to this very day.

# The Fox and the Stork

**A** fox and a stork were once friends. One day, the fox invited the stork to dinner — but he thought it would be funny to serve the meal in shallow bowls. The fox could easily lap up his soup, but the stork could not reach hers with her long bill. She left as hungry as when she arrived.

"I'm sorry," said the fox, laughing to himself, "that the soup is not to your liking."

"Do not apologise," said the stork, and they fixed a date when the fox would go for dinner at the stork's house.

When the day came, the stork served soup in a tall, thin jug. The fox couldn't reach any of the delicious soup but the stork could easily fit her long, thin bill inside.

"I will not apologise," said the stork. "One bad turn deserves another."

# Nasreddin Hodja
## and the Pot

**N**asreddin Hodja went to his neighbour to borrow a large cooking pot. When he returned it, the neighbour was surprised to find a smaller pot inside.

"What's this, Nasreddin?" he said.

"Oh, your pot gave birth while in my house," Nasreddin replied, "and naturally as the larger pot is yours, the smaller pot belongs to you also."

'What a fool!' thought the man, but he smiled and accepted the pot.

Some days later, Nasreddin asked if he might borrow the pot again. After a few weeks, the neighbour went to ask for it back.

"Oh, I am sorry to tell you," said Nasreddin, "but your pot has died."

"Don't be so foolish" said the neighbour angrily. "Cooking pots don't die!"

"Are you sure?" said Nasreddin. "You didn't seem surprised when you heard it had given birth."

# How the Town Became a Lake

**O**nce upon a time, there was a town where there is now a lake. Its streets were full of beautiful houses and at the centre was a magnificent church. On Sundays, the golden bells in the church steeple and the songs of the choir rose to the mountains that surrounded the town.

But life was too easy for the people who lived there. They grew to care only about pleasure and forgot to look after the sick, the old and the feeble.

One day, a terrible thing happened. Water began to rise above the paving stones of the streets and to wash about the feet of the careless people. The water rose and rose until there was no town left! Instead there was a still lake, cradled by mountains. Sometimes, you can still hear bells ringing beneath the water.

# A Silly Question

Dolly asked her little kitten, "How did you come to be white when all your brothers are tabby?"

"Well," the kitten began, "When we were small we hunted mice every night. One night I came to a hole I had never noticed before. I crept through it and found myself in a room. There was cheese, fish, cream, mice and milk. It was the happiest hour of my life. At the end, as I was washing, I noticed that on nails around the room were fur coats. I stood rooted to the ground and suddenly a terrible monster stood before me. In less than a moment it had hung my tabby fur coat on a nail behind the door. I had to creep out of that lovely fairyland without a fur coat. And that's how I came to be white."

"I don't quite see —" began Dolly.

"No? Why, what would your mother do if someone took away your coat?"

"Buy me another, I suppose."

"Exactly. But when my mother took me to the cat coat shop, they were out of tabby coats in my size, so I had to have a white one."

# Simple Simon in London

**Simple Simon** had lived all his life in the country, but one day he decided to visit London. As he was walking around, a dog ran out of a house and snapped at Simple Simon, who bent down to pick up a stone to throw at the dog. But he found them all cemented in as cobblestones.

"What a strange place London is," he said. "In the country we keep our dogs tied up and our stones loose, but here they keep their dogs loose and tie up their stones."

# The Man and the Wooden God

**Long ago,** people used to worship statues. They would pray to them for luck and good fortune, and give offerings of food, wine and flowers.

There was a man who often prayed to a wooden statue. But no matter how hard he prayed, and no matter what offerings he left, his luck never changed. One day, he became frustrated with the statue's silence. In a temper, he swept it down from its pedestal. The statue broke in two, and gold coins streamed from inside it.

"Ah!" the delighted man cried. "You do have some use after all!"

# The Gingerbread Man

**O**ne day, **an old woman made** a gingerbread man. But while she was waiting for him to cool, he hopped off the baking tray and ran out of the door! The old woman ran after him. "Run, run, as fast as you can! You can't catch me, I'm the gingerbread man!" he called.

The gingerbread man ran so fast that the old woman couldn't catch him. Her husband and their cat and dog joined the chase — but they couldn't catch him either.

The gingerbread man ran on and on until he came to a river, and then he had to stop. "How can I get across?" he wailed.

A sly fox suddenly appeared by his side and said, "Jump on my nose — I'll swim you across."

But as soon as the gingerbread man jumped on the fox's nose — *SNAP!* The fox gobbled him up.

# The Hut in the Forest

There were once two sisters who lived with their parents in a hut on the edge of a forest. Their father was a woodcutter, and one of his daughters would bring him lunch every day. One day his youngest daughter was bringing the lunch when she lost her way in the forest.

She wandered for hours, until she came to a little house and knocked on the door. A voice cried, "Come in."

When she opened the door, an old man was sitting at a table. Three animals — a hen, a cockerel and a cow — were nearby. When the girl asked to stay the night the old man replied, "You can, but first you must cook our meal."

The girl prepared dinner for two — but she didn't think of feeding the animals. And when she and the grey-haired man had finished eating, a trapdoor opened beneath her

chair and the girl landed in the cold cellar with a bump!

The next day, the girl's older sister set out to find her. She too found the hut in the forest, and the old man said the same thing to her. The sister fed the cockerel, cow and hen. Then she made dinner for the grey-haired man and herself. The old man thanked her and showed her to a tiny room where she could spend the night.

In the morning the girl was woken by a bright flash. She got up to see what had happened. In the dawn light the house seemed much grander than it had the night before, and she met a handsome prince on the stairs. He explained that he was the old man. "A witch enchanted me and my servants. The spell could only be broken by someone whose heart is full of love for all living things."

They rescued the younger sister from the cellar, and she was delighted to learn that her sister and the prince had fallen in love. They were soon married and lived happily ever after.

# The Ugly Duckling

**O**ne day a batch of duck eggs hatched in a farmyard. Strangely, one chick was much bigger and uglier than the rest. The poor duckling was pecked and pushed about by all the other ducks — and the chickens too. "He's too big — and so ugly!" they clucked. The duckling was very sad, so he ran away.

He spent the whole winter alone. Then one day he looked down at his reflection in the water and saw he was no longer a grey, ugly duckling — he was a swan! He held his neck high and swam over to some other swans, who were calling to him. "I never dreamt I could be so happy when I was the ugly duckling!" he cried.

# The Crow

**O**nce there was a princess who loved to walk in the garden of a ruined castle. One day, a black crow hopped out and said, "I am a prince under a witch's spell. Will you help me, Princess? To do so you must live in this ruined castle by yourself, and if anything frightening happens you must not scream."

The kind princess agreed to help, and hurried into the castle. At midnight a troop of goblins, sprites, imps, witches and trolls burst in. They lit a fire, placed a cauldron of water on it, and dragged the princess towards the cauldron. But the brave princess did not utter a sound. Just as she reached the cauldron the evil spirits vanished.

For nine days the princess sat alone in the castle, and for nine nights she kept her word and remained silent, no matter what scary things happened.

On the tenth day, she heard a rustle of wings as the crow returned. He turned into a prince before her eyes, and said, "By your kindness, you have freed me. Will you stay with me always?"

The princess agreed, and when she looked around she found the castle ruins transformed — it was now bright and beautiful, filled with fine furniture and cheerful servants. And there they lived for many happy years.

# A Day's Work

**A** man once made a deal with a mean goblin that he hoped would make him very rich: if the man could find a job the goblin couldn't finish, the goblin would give him all his gold. If he failed, he would have to give the goblin everything he owned. The goblin appeared at the man's house, and asked, "What's my work?"

The man threw ten thousand seeds over a nearby field, and said, "You must pick up every seed!"

This was an easy task for the goblin, and he soon returned to ask for a new task. The man took the goblin to a beach and told him to sweep up all the sand. The goblin did as he was asked. Soon the man was in despair! His wife, however, had an idea, and she took one curly hair from her head, "Tell him to straighten this hair," she said.

All day long the goblin tried, but he couldn't do it – and so the man was saved by his wife's cleverness.

# The Two Neighbours

Long ago, two neighbours prayed to the great god Zeus. The god saw that one of the neighbours had a terrible greed for money and that the other neighbour was always envious. So, to teach them both a lesson, Zeus decided that he would grant each man whatever he wished, but the other neighbour would get twice as much.

The first greedy neighbour wished for a room filled with gold and was amazed when it appeared before him! A few minutes later the second neighbour came to boast that two rooms of gold had appeared in his house.

The second neighbour was instantly envious that the first neighbour had gold too, even though he had twice as much himself. So he wished that his neighbour might lose his room of gold. Of course, it was no sooner said than done – but he himself lost both his rooms of gold.

# How the Hedgehog Beat the Hare

**A** hedgehog once bet a hare that he could run for longer than him. The hare agreed to the contest. The two met in a ditch, and the hedgehog explained they would run from one side to the other, until one of them gave up.

They took up their positions on one side of the ditch and set off. But the hare did not know that the hedgehog had asked a friend to hide on the other side of the ditch, and when the first hedgehog reached the other side, his friend took over. The crafty hedgehogs repeated this until the hare could run no more. "You win!" he puffed.

# Anansi Finds some Meat

**W**hen mother hyena was away, Anansi the trick-
playing spider went to the hyena's den. He told the
hyena's cubs that he was their uncle, called You-all. "Wake
me when your mother brings food," he said, and he went
to sleep.

Mother hyena soon came home with some meat, which
she gave to her cubs, saying, "This is for you all."

So the cubs woke Anansi and gave him the meat, which
he gobbled up. Mother hyena brought meat twice more,
saying, "This is for you all." And each time, the cubs gave
Anansi the meat.

In the evening when mother hyena came home, the cubs
started crying for food.

"How are you still hungry after all the meat I gave you?"
she asked, surprised.

"Uncle ate it all!" they
wailed.

'Time to go!' thought
Anansi. And he
sprinted away, very
happy with his
many meals.

# Raggedy Ann and the Kittens

**Raggedy Ann, the rag doll,** and the other toys were sitting in the nursery when Fido the dog came in.

"Guess what!" said Fido. "I went into the barn to hunt for mice, and found three tiny kittens in an old basket in a dark corner!"

The toys could hardly wait until it was time for bed that night. Raggedy Ann suggested that all the dolls go down to the barn and see the kittens. This they did easily, for the window was open and it was only a short jump to the ground.

The dolls crawled through the hole in the barn door and ran to the basket. Just as Raggedy Ann reached down to pick up one of the kittens there was a lot of howling and yelping, and Fido came bounding through the hole with Mamma Cat hissing behind him.

"I'm surprised at you, Mamma Cat!" said Raggedy Ann, "Fido wouldn't hurt your kittens for anything!"

"I'm sorry, then," said Mamma Cat.

"Have you told the folks up at the house about your kittens?" Raggedy Ann asked.

"Oh, my, no!" exclaimed Mamma Cat.

"Let's take them into the house!" said Raggedy Ann, "and Mistress can find them there in the morning!"

"How lovely!" said all the dolls. "Do take them to the house, Mamma Cat!"

So Raggedy Ann carried two of the kittens to the house while Mamma Cat carried the other. Fido insisted that Mamma Cat and the kittens should take over his nice, soft basket.

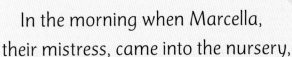

In the morning when Marcella, their mistress, came into the nursery, the first thing she saw were the three little kittens. She cried out in delight, and carried them off to show her Mamma and Daddy.

Mamma and Daddy said Marcella could keep the kittens, and she eventually decided upon three names – Prince Charming for the white kitten, Cinderella for the grey tabby and Princess Golden for the kitten with the yellow stripes. So that is how the three little kittens came to live in the nursery.

And Mamma Cat found out that Fido was a very good friend, too. She grew to trust him so much she would even let him help wash the kittens' faces.

# The Fighting Birds and the Partridge

**A** man who kept poultry had two fighting cockerels among his birds. One day, by chance, he found a tame partridge for sale. He bought it and took it home to be reared with the cockerels. However, when the partridge was put into the poultry yard, the cockerels flew at it and followed it about, and the partridge became distressed.

Of course, the partridge thought that the cockerels were treating him so badly because he was a stranger. Yet not long afterwards, he saw them fighting each other. They fought furiously, and did not quit until one had well and truly beaten the other. Then the partridge said to himself, "I won't get upset at being bullied by these birds, for they even quarrel with each other."

# King Thrushbeard

There was once a princess who was beautiful, but unkind. One day she told her father to find her a prince to marry. The king invited kings from near and far to visit the palace — but the princess mocked them all. "He's too lanky," she said. "He's too squat...", "That one's so dull..." She even laughed at a king with a bushy beard, "You should be called King Thrushbeard!"

The king was angry that his daughter was so rude, and told her that she must marry the next person who arrived. This turned out to be a musician, coming to play in the hope of earning a few coins. The princess fumed, but she had to obey the king.

Her new husband led her away down the road, and as they walked they passed a large town. "This town belongs to King Thrushbeard," said the musician.

The princess sighed, "I should never have been so rude to him!"

When they came to the little hut where the musician lived, he taught the princess to tend the fire and cook the food. He was very kind, and she felt pleased when she had learnt how to do it all.

A few days later the musician said, "I cannot earn enough for both of us to live on. You must go and work in King Thrushbeard's palace as a kitchen maid."

So the princess did. Even though she had to do the dirtiest, most unpleasant jobs, she felt pride that she was earning money to look after herself and her husband.

One day, the palace buzzed with the news that King Thrushbeard was getting married. Guests arrived in beautiful clothes. After a busy morning in the kitchen, the princess went to the ballroom to get a peek of the grand wedding feast laid out on the tables.

She was astonished when King Thrushbeard himself saw her and took her hand. "It is me," he said. "I disguised myself as a musician in order to teach you a lesson."

The princess apologised to him. "I should never have been so proud and rude!"

The king took her hands in his and said, "It is all forgotten... and now it is time for us to get married properly."

The princess was dressed in a beautiful gown, and her father and all his royal court arrived to celebrate the joyful wedding day.

# The Lad and the Devil

**O**ne day a lad was walking along a road cracking nuts, when he met the Devil.

"Is it true," said the lad, "that you can climb into a nut hole?"

"Certainly," said the Devil.

"Then just creep into this nut," said the lad.

So the Devil did.

Now, when he had crept well in, the lad sealed up the nut with a pin.

Then the lad came to a blacksmith, and asked if he'd crack that nut for him.

"That I will," said the blacksmith, and he took his hammer and gave the nut a huge blow.

The nut flew into pieces with such a bang that half the roof blew off. "Why! I think the Devil was in that nut," said the blacksmith.

"He was, you're quite right," said the lad, and went away laughing.

# The Drop of Water

Once there was an old man called Cribble-Crabble, who loved using his microscope to look at tiny things.

One day, he looked at a drop of muddy water through the microscope.

What a sight he saw! The water was actually filled with teeny-tiny creepy-crawly creatures. They wriggled and squirmed and crawled all over each other. It even looked as though some of them were fighting!

Cribble-Crabble called his next-door neighbour, who was a magician, to come in. He looked through the microscope and gasped.

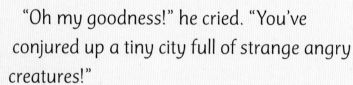

"Oh my goodness!" he cried. "You've conjured up a tiny city full of strange angry creatures!"

"No!" cried Cribble-Crabble. "It's a drop of muddy water."

The magician couldn't decide whether the microscope was science or magic.

# The Goose that Laid the Golden Eggs

**O**nce upon a time, there lived a farmer who owned a prize goose. One morning, when the farmer went to check the goose's nest, he found an unusual egg — it was bright yellow, shiny, and very heavy. When the farmer examined it closely, he realized it was made of pure gold.

The next day the goose laid another golden egg, and the next day, and the next. The farmer was soon on his way to being wealthy.

However, as he grew richer, he also became greedier. He thought the goose must have a huge lump of gold inside it and he wanted it all at once, so he decided to kill it.

Of course, inside he found no gold at all. In his wish to have a huge fortune in one go, the farmer lost his chance to gain a little every day.

# Why the Swallow's Tail is Forked

The Great Spirit once asked all the animals that he had made to come to him. "How can I make life better?"

Man stepped forwards and said, "The serpent feasts upon my blood. Will you give him other food instead?"

"The serpent must eat," said the Great Spirit. "Mosquito, find out which creature's blood is best for the serpent."

The mosquito travelled over the earth and on his way bit every creature he could to find whose blood was the best. On his way back, he looked up and saw a swallow.

"I'm glad to see you, my friend," sang the swallow. "Have you found out whose blood is best for the serpent?"

"The blood of man," answered the mosquito.

The swallow had always been a friend of man, and he wanted to help him, so he pecked the mosquito's tongue!

When the Great Spirit asked the mosquito whose blood was best, the mosquito could not speak. Then the swallow said, "Great Father, I met the mosquito before we arrived here and he told me frog's blood is best for the serpent."

The serpent was angry — he didn't like frog's blood. So, next time the swallow flew near him, he bit a piece from the middle of his tail.

# Sir Gammer Vans

Last Sunday morning at six o'clock in the evening as I was sailing over the mountains in my little boat, I visited Sir Gammer Vans. He lives in a brick house, built entirely of flint, standing alone by itself in the middle of sixty others. In the garden is an apple tree made of iron, covered in steel pears. He gave me a slice of beer, and a cup of veal.

Then, we went out and saw eighteen birds, besides a dead salmon that was flying over the bridge, out of which I made the best apple pie I ever tasted.

# The Man and the Eagle

An eagle was once captured by a man, who clipped his wings and put him in the poultry yard, along with the chickens. The eagle was very depressed about his change in fortune.

"Why should you be so sad?" said the man. "When you were an eagle, you were just ordinary but as a rooster, you're the finest one I ever saw."

# The Thirsty Pigeon

There was once a pigeon who had flown for many miles without water. She was desperate for a drink, but could not find a pond or even a puddle to sip from.

Then she saw what she thought was a goblet of water, so she flew towards it excitedly. *BANG!* She crashed right into a signboard — the goblet was just painted on it. The pigeon slid to the ground, her head spinning. "Enthusiasm should not outweigh caution," she sighed.

# The Doll in the Grass

**O**nce upon a time there was a king
who had twelve sons. One day he
told them all to find themselves wives who
could make a shirt in one day.

When the youngest son, Ashiepattle,
went to seek a wife, he found a tiny doll in
the grass. She looked very beautiful. He told
her his tale and said, "If you can make a shirt,
will you become my wife?"

She said that she would, and set to work spinning and
weaving. Soon she had made a beautiful shirt, and
Ashiepattle returned home and showed it to the king. The
king was pleased with it, so Ashiepattle set out to fetch his
bride. When he arrived to collect her, she said she would
travel in a silver spoon, drawn by two small white mice!

When they had travelled a short way they came to a
large lake. The little doll jumped into the water! Ashiepattle
was just about to dive in to look for her when a merman
brought her up to the surface. In front of Ashiepattle's eyes
the doll grew until she was human-sized!

They rode the rest of the way to the palace together on
Ashiepattle's horse. There they were married, and lived
happily ever after.

# The Troll and the Bear

**O**nce upon a time there was a troll who travelled to a farm in Norway every Christmas Eve. When he arrived he would make everyone leave the house, and sit by the fire eating frogs.

Then, one year, a man with a performing bear also arrived at the farm. The farmer told him about the troll but the man begged to be allowed to stay. Towards the evening, the troll came and sat down by the fire. The man pinched the bear's paw and the bear growled.

"Take care," said the man to the troll, "or he'll tear you into pieces."

The troll looked frightened and asked, "Are there more like him?"

"Yes," said the man, "but the others are much fiercer. They're on their way now."

The troll thought that he wouldn't much like to tackle more than one bear, so he left in a hurry and has never shown himself since.

# The Dog and his Reflection

**O**nce upon a time a dog found a piece of meat and decided to carry it home in his mouth to eat in peace. After a while he came across a stream and trotted along beside it.

As the dog walked along he looked down at the water, then stopped in surprise. There was another dog with a piece of meat looking up at him from the water! The dog had no idea it was his own reflection. His only thought was that he had to have the other piece of meat too. He made a snap at the dog in the water, but as he opened his mouth he dropped the meat. It plopped into the stream and sank!

# Lazy Jack

There was once a boy who was known as Lazy Jack. He never did any work, until one day his mother told him to go and work for the neighbouring farmer. At the end of the day the farmer paid him with a wheel of cheese. Jack carried it home in his hat, which he put on his head. By the time he got home it had melted.

"You should have held it in your hands," said his mother, shaking her head.

The next day the farmer paid Jack with a cat. Jack carried the cat home in his hands but it scratched until he let go, so he lost it. When he got home, his mother said, "You should have walked it home on a string."

"I'll do so another time," said Jack.

The next day, the farmer gave Jack a leg of lamb as payment. Jack tied it to a string, and trailed it along after him in the dirt, so that by the time he got home it was completely spoilt.

"You silly boy!" said his mother, "You should have carried it on your shoulder."

"I'll do so another time," replied Jack.

The day after, the farmer gave Jack a donkey. So with some trouble Jack hoisted the donkey onto his shoulder and started walking home. Now, it just so happened that Jack's way home passed a house where a rich man lived with his daughter, who could not hear or speak. The doctors said she would be cured if she could be made to laugh. The girl saw Jack passing by, with the donkey, kicking and hee-hawing on his shoulders, and she burst into great fits of laughter. At once her speech and hearing returned! Her father was overjoyed, and let her marry Lazy Jack, who was made a rich gentleman. They lived in a large house, and Jack's mother lived with them in great happiness.

# The Khoja's Robe

One day the Khoja's wife washed his robe and hung it on a tree branch to dry in the garden of the house. That night when the Khoja went out, he thought he saw a robber climbing down the tree. He shouted to his wife, "Quick, give me my bow and arrows!"

Then he went outside and shot at the robe, piercing it through and through. The Khoja returned to the house, happy he had dealt with the burglar. The next morning, he discovered that it was his own robe he had shot at, and exclaimed, "What a narrow escape! If I had been wearing my robe as usual, I would have shot myself!"

# The Crow and the Serpent

**A** **very hungry crow** was fast using up the little energy he had in looking for food. At last he spotted a serpent asleep in a sunny nook. Swooping down, he seized it greedily in his beak.

But the serpent struck out with his fangs and bit the crow. The crow dropped the serpent and flapped away to find some other, less dangerous, meal. "What seems to be a blessing may not always be the case!" he screeched.

# Tom Thumb

**A** poor woodcutter and his wife had a teeny-tiny baby boy, who grew up to be no bigger than a thumb, so they called him Tom Thumb. Small as he was, the couple loved him dearly. Tom was good and thoughtful, and helped his parents as best he could.

One day, Tom went to help his father cart logs. On the way home he sat on the horse's head, right by its ear, giving it directions. Two men were passing, and they saw Tom and thought they could show him at fairs for money and make their fortune. They waited until the woodcutter wasn't looking, then one of the men grabbed Tom and put him in his pocket. After a while the two men stopped to rest. As soon they sat down, Tom snuck out of the pocket and hid in a snail shell until the men moved on again. Then he started to walk the long, long way home.

As darkness fell, a wolf crept up on Tom and threatened to eat him, but Tom thought quickly came up with a plan.

"My friend," he said, "You shouldn't eat me, for I know where many more tasty treats than just me can be found."

"Tell me more," growled the wolf.

So Tom described his parents' cottage. "When we reach it, you can crawl through the drain into the kitchen, and then into the pantry," he suggested. "There you will find ham, beef, cold chicken, roast pig, cakes, apple cider, and everything that your heart can wish for."

So Tom climbed on the wolf's back to show him the way and the wolf sped off to the woodcutter's cottage. The wolf crawled through the drain into the kitchen and into the pantry. There he ate and drank to his heart's content. But when he tried to squeeze back out through the drain, his stomach was now so big and full that he would not fit, no matter how hard he tried.

That was just what Tom had counted on, and now he began to shout at the top of his voice, "Father! Mother! It's me, Tom! I'm in the pantry with a wolf."

The woodcutter and his wife awoke at once and went down to the kitchen. The woodcutter chased the wolf out of his house, and they all lived happily ever after.

# The Fox and the Grapes

**A** **fox was strolling** through an orchard when he noticed a bunch of juicy grapes. The fox licked his lips. "Those delicious grapes would be just the thing to quench my thirst," he said to himself. But the only problem was, he couldn't reach them.

Nevertheless, the fox was determined to have the grapes for himself. He jumped as high as he could, but missed. Again and again he jumped and tried to reach the grapes, until he was quite worn out. All the creatures in the orchard were laughing.

At last, the fox had to admit defeat and gave up. As he walked away to the sound of sniggering, he stuck his nose in the air and said, "I am sure those grapes are sour, anyway."

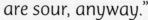

# The Problem of the Gordian Knot

The people of Phrygia had a great wonder — an ox-cart tied to a pole with a wonderfully intricate knot of dried bark. It had been said that anyone who could untie the knot would become king of all Asia. But how could anyone undo it when the bark was too brittle to be moved, and the ends were tucked somewhere in the middle of the knot?

Many men considered the problem but no one could do it. Then the greatest warrior of the ancient world, Alexander, came riding into town with his army. He was told the story, and demanded to be taken to the knot. "This is how I solve the puzzle!" he declared, and taking his sword he sliced the knot in two. Ever since, cutting the Gordian knot means finding a simple solution to an impossible problem.

# The Sheep and the Pig

**O**nce there was a big sheep who lived on a farm, and one morning the farmer said to his wife, "Let's eat that sheep tomorrow."

The big sheep heard these words, and was scared, so he went and told the pig the news.

"Let's run away to the woods," the pig said. "I can chop trees and we can build a house together."

So off they went. When they had gone a little way, a hare ran up to them.

"Good-day," said the sheep. "We're going to build a house in the woods."

"I'll go with you," said the hare, "I have teeth to gnaw pegs, and paws to hammer them. I'll be the carpenter."

So they set off to the woods to build the house. The pig cut the logs, the sheep pulled them home and the hare put them together.

And they all lived happily together because there is no place like home.

# The Three Dolls

The Sultan of Persia was one of the wisest men in his kingdom and there was nothing he loved more than solving puzzles. One day, a parcel arrived and inside the box lay three wooden dolls with a note: *'Tell these three dolls apart.'*

He looked at them. They were exactly the same, even the pattern of the wood was the same. The Sultan knew he needed to consult an expert, but no one could help.

Finally, his storyteller stepped forward and pulled a hair from the Sultan's beard. She inserted it into the ear of the first doll. It disappeared into the head of the doll. "Hmm," said the storyteller. "This doll is like a wise person – everything he hears goes into his head and stays there."

The storyteller put another hair into the ear of the second doll. It came out the other side. "This doll is like a fool – everything it hears goes in one ear and out the other."

The storyteller pushed a third hair into the ear of the third doll. It went further and further in. It came, twisted, out of the lips.

"Why, this doll is the storyteller. What it hears goes in, and gets retold with a small twist. For every storyteller changes the story just a little to make it his own."

# The Bat and the Weasels

**O**ne evening, a bat flew straight into a tree and fell to the ground. Before the bat could fly away again, a weasel caught him.

The bat begged to be released but the weasel said he couldn't do that because he was an enemy of the birds. "I'm not a bird, I'm a mouse," said the bat.

The weasel looked at the bat. "So you are," he said, and he let the bat go.

Soon after, the bat was caught in the same way by another weasel, and begged for his life.

"No," said the weasel, "I never let a mouse go."

"I'm not a mouse," said the bat, "I'm a bird."

The weasel examined the bat. "So you are," he said, and he too let the bat go.

# The Two Frogs

In Japan there lived two frogs, one in the town of Osaka, the other in Kyoto. One day, each frog decided to visit the other's town. In the middle of their journeys was a mountain, which they both climbed.

Now, although the frogs' noses pointed forwards, their eyes were so positioned that each could only see behind him. From the top of the mountain, the frogs thought that the town they were to visit looked exactly like the one from which they had come. So both gave up their journeys.

# Tikki Tikki Tembo

Two brothers were playing near a well when one of the brothers, named Tikki Tikki Tembo No Sarimbo Hari Kari Bushkie Perry Pem Do Hai Kai Pom Pom Nikki No Meeno Dom Barako, fell in.

His brother shouted, "Help! Tikki Tikki Tembo No Sarimbo Hari Kari Bushkie Perry Pem Do Hai Kai Pom Pom Nikki No Meeno Dom Barako has fallen into the well!" But it took so long to shout, that the boy was half-drowned by the time the gardener came and fished him out. So after that everyone agreed to just call him 'Tembo'.

# Finding Raggedy Andy

One day, Daddy took Raggedy Ann down to his office and propped her up against some books on his desk. He wanted to have her where he could see her cheery smile all day.

Just as Daddy was finishing his day's work, a package arrived. Daddy opened it and found a letter from Grandma, which said that at the time Raggedy Ann was made, a neighbour had made a boy doll called Raggedy Andy, which she enclosed.

His soft, floppy arms were folded up in front of him, and his legs were folded over his arms. They were held this way by a rubber band.

After slipping off the rubber band, Daddy smoothed out the wrinkles in Raggedy Andy's arms and legs. Then he propped Raggedy Ann and Raggedy Andy up against books on his desk, so they sat facing each other — Raggedy Ann's shoe button eyes looking straight into the shoe button eyes of Raggedy Andy.

They could not speak to each other in front of Daddy — so they just sat there and smiled at each other. "So, Raggedy Ann and Raggedy Andy," said Daddy, "I will go away and let you get reacquainted."

Daddy then took the rubber band and placed it around Raggedy Ann's right hand, and around Raggedy Andy's right hand.

Daddy knew they would like to tell each other all the wonderful things that had happened since they had parted more than fifty years ago, so he left them alone.

The next morning, when Daddy unlocked his door, he saw that Raggedy Andy had fallen over so that he lay with his head cuddled into the bend of Raggedy Ann's arm.

# The All Dog

A lion once saw a poodle and, very rudely, burst into laughter at how ridiculous he looked.

"Whoever saw so small a beast?" said the lion.

"It is very true," said the poodle, with dignity, "that I am small; but, sir, I have to point out that you are only a largish type of cat. I am all dog."

# The Man and his Wives

**L**ong, long ago, it was the custom for a man to have many wives. In these times, there was a middle-aged man who had two wives — one old and one young.

Now there came a time when the man's hair began to turn grey. The young wife did not like this at all as she thought it made him look too old. Every night she combed his hair and picked out all the grey ones.

However, the older wife was pleased that her husband was going grey. This was because people had sometimes mistaken her for his mother! Every morning, she combed the man's hair and picked out the brown ones.

Of course, there was only one result — the man soon ended up entirely bald!

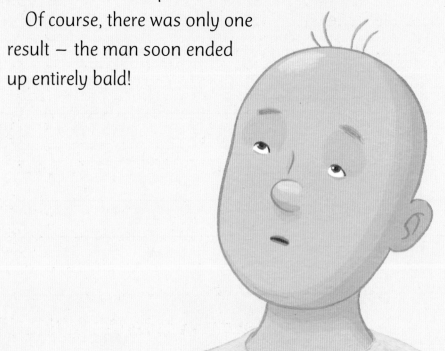

# The Jumpers

**O**nce upon a time, a flea, a grasshopper and a goose
decided to hold a jumping competition against each
other. The king said he would give his daughter's hand in
marriage to the creature who jumped the highest.

The flea jumped first — and he went so high that
nobody could see him. The grasshopper only jumped half
as high as the flea.

The goose stood still for a long time. Then all of a
sudden the court dog gave him a nudge and — *PLOP!* he
jumped sideways, straight
into the lap of the princess.

"Splendid!" cried the king.
"To jump up to my daughter is
the highest jump that can be
made. It takes brains to get an
idea like that — and the goose has
shown that he does have brains."

So the jumping goose won
the princess.

# Little Topknot

A cockerel and some hens lived in a farmyard. One hen had a pretty topknot that she was very proud of, so she strutted about a lot.

One day she said, "I'm tired of this farmyard. I want the world to see me. I shall fly over the fence."

The cockerel said, "Don't go!"

All the old hens said, "Don't go-go-go!"

But little Topknot flew over the fence and carried on strutting down the road.

Just then a hawk flew over her head. He saw little Topknot all alone, so he flew down and caught her in his claws! The farmer came running and frightened the hawk away, but the hawk had scratched her pretty topknot with his claws.

Little Topknot was glad to get back to the farmyard. And now she doesn't strut about, but scratches for seeds like the rest.

# The Fisherman and the Bottle

**A** **poor fisherman** went out in his boat one morning and caught nothing but a strange brass bottle, sealed with a cork. Curiously, he tugged at the cork and opened the bottle. At that moment, smoke came out of the bottle, and quickly formed itself into the shape of a huge genie.

"At last I am free!" it roared, "Now I will punish you!"

The fisherman thought quickly. "That's a fancy trick, the way you came out of that bottle," he said. "I bet you couldn't ever get back into it."

"Of course I could," said the Genie.

"Prove it," said the fisherman and the Genie coiled himself back into the small bottle.

Quickly the fisherman rammed the cork in, and threw the bottle back into the sea.

# Jupiter and the Tortoise

**L**ong ago, when the great god Jupiter ruled the Earth, the time came for him to marry. Jupiter invited all the animals to the wedding. The day arrived, the ceremony was performed, and then everyone gathered for the banquet. Jupiter noticed that one animal was missing — the tortoise. The feast was a success, but Jupiter was sad that the tortoise had not turned up, so he went to ask him why.

"I don't care for going out," said the tortoise, "there's no place like home."

Jupiter was enraged by this reply, and declared that from then on the tortoise should carry his house on his back — so he would never be able to get away from his home, even if he wished to.

# The Darning Needle

There was once a **darning needle** who saw
itself as special. One day the cook used
the needle to mend a slipper and its tip broke
off. The cook used the broken needle to pin her
shawl together. "I'm a beautiful brooch!" boasted
the needle.

The next day the needle fell off the shawl into the street.
A boy picked it up and stuck it in a eggshell to make a
boat with a mast. "I'm so important," the needle cried.

But the next moment — *CRACK!* A bicycle ran over the
eggshell. The darning needle shattered into tiny pieces, and
learnt that it wasn't so beautiful and important after all.

# The Top and the Ball

A **spinning top** and a ball lay together in a box. "Shall we
be married, as we live together?" said the top. But the
ball thought a lot of herself and would not even reply.

The next day, a little boy came along. He painted the top
red and yellow so that while it was spinning around it
looked quite splendid.

The day after, the ball was taken out by the boy. The top

watched the ball bouncing high in the air like a bird, but then the boy lost it on a great big bounce. He searched everywhere for the ball, but it could not be found.

Several years passed by, and the top was no longer young — so the boy painted him a beautiful gold colour. From time to time the spinning top thought of the ball that he once loved.

But then one day the top spun out of control, and he too was lost. He had fallen into a dustbin, where all sorts of rubbish lay about along with dust, leaves and other things.

"Now I am in a fix," he said. Then he glanced at a curious round thing, like an old apple, which lay nearby. It was the ball, which had lain for years in the gutter and now was soaked through with water. Looking at it, the top realized he no longer loved the proud ball.

The next day a woman came to clean out the dustbin. "Ah," she exclaimed, "here is the spinning top." So the top was taken back into the house, but nothing more was heard of the ball.

# Hercules and the Waggoner

**A**waggoner was carefully driving his heavy cart along when the wheels sank in the mud. He set his shoulder to the cart and urged the horse forwards, but the wheels only sank deeper.

The waggoner prayed to the ancient hero Hercules, who was famous for his great strength.

"Hercules, please help me!" he cried.

"You called?" came a booming voice.

The waggoner spun around to see a giant of a man, with a lion skin wrapped round his shoulders. Hercules — for it was he — said, "Don't just stand there. I'm not going to do it for you! Set your shoulder to the wheel for one more push, and this time I'll help."

# The Turtle's Rescue

There were once four animals that were great friends — a deer, a crow, a turtle, and a mouse.

One day, a man captured the turtle, tied him up, and set off towards his home. The three remaining friends quickly made a plan to set the turtle free. The deer lay down in the road, pretending to be hurt. The crow even pretended to peck at his head. The mouse hid nearby and waited.

The man saw the deer as he travelled along the road. He set down the turtle so his hands were free to collect the deer. But as the man approached, the crow flew away, and the deer got to its feet and ran off!

Cursing his bad luck, the man went back to get the turtle, but he found that it too had disappeared. The mouse had chewed through its ropes! And so the four friends were reunited.

# The Miller with the Golden Thumb

An unkind merchant said to a miller, "I have heard that every honest miller has a golden thumb. Please, let me see your thumb." And when the miller showed it to him, the merchant said, "I can't see that your thumb is gold. It is the same as other men's thumbs!"

The miller answered, "My thumb is gold, but you will not be able to see it, for it looks like an ordinary thumb to a fool." Well, that silenced the merchant!

# The Boy and the Fox

A boy saw a fox asleep on a hillside. He looked at it for a little while, thinking, then said out loud, "I'll catch this fox and sell it. I'll buy wheat seed with the money, and sow them in my father's field. The people who pass by will see my wheat and they'll say, 'What fine wheat that boy has'. Then I'll say to them, 'Keep OUT of my wheat field!'

But the boy shouted this last bit so loudly that the fox woke with a start, and had disappeared into the woods before the boy could even grasp one of its hairs.

# The Glass Chest

There was once a young man who decided to go travelling, but he soon became lost in a great forest. He was just starting to worry when a stag bounded up to him, swept him up on its great antlers, and carried him away to a huge mountain cave.

The cave contained many bottles filled with blue gas, and in the middle stood two glass chests. In the first chest was a model of a tiny castle, surrounded by a miniature village. Inside the second chest lay a beautiful young woman! Suddenly she opened her eyes. "Oh, thank goodness!" she cried. "Please help me out of this prison."

The man hurried to release her.

"I am the daughter of a rich nobleman," she explained. "One evening a stranger came and asked to marry me. I refused him and he cast a spell to trap me in this glass chest. He changed my brother into a stag and shrank my castle and village, putting them into the other glass chest.

He turned all my people into smoke and trapped them in bottles, and then put me into a deep, enchanted sleep. But at last, you have set me free! Please help me carry the glass chest with my castle outside."

Once they were outside, they opened the chest and watched the castle and village quickly grow back to full size.

Next, the young woman opened the bottles. The blue smoke rushed out and became people. Everyone was overjoyed!

Then a handsome young man came striding out of the forest. It was the noblewoman's brother! He told them that after he had delivered the young man to his sister, he had found and fought the evil magician. The magician had fled, and the enchantment was lifted — so he had been returned to his true form.

And on that very day, the beautiful noblewoman married the young man who had saved her, and they lived happily ever after in the castle.

# The Horse and his Rider

**A** **young man** fancied himself as a good rider, so one market day he looked for a horse to buy. He found one he liked and was determined to ride it.

Unfortunately he did not know enough about horses to know that this horse had not been broken in, and he didn't think to ask. He climbed straight onto its back, and the second the horse felt a weight in the saddle, it set off at full gallop.

One of the rider's friends saw him thundering down the road. Surprised, he called out, "Where are you off to in such a hurry?"

Gasping for breath, the young man pointed to the horse and replied, "No idea – you will have to ask him."

# The Swineherd

**A** **prince longed to marry** an emperor's daughter, so he sent her two presents – a rose and a songbird. He heard back that the princess was not impressed by the gifts, but the prince was not put off. He decided that he must meet her, and took a job as the emperor's swineherd.

While he watched the pigs, the prince made a metal cooking pot with bells on it. When the pot boiled, the bells played, and allowed you to smell the food being cooked in every home in the city.

The princess sent a maid to find out where the sound was coming from. When the maid returned and told the princess about the swineherd's magic pot, the princess declared she must have it. But the maid said, "The swineherd said the price of the pot is ten kisses." So the princess gave the swineherd ten kisses for the pot.

Next the swineherd made a magic rattle that played any music ever composed when it was shaken. This time the maid reported that the swineherd wanted a hundred kisses for it! The princess agreed, but the emperor passed by and saw what was going on. He was furious at the very idea that his daughter would kiss a lowly swineherd.

The next morning, the prince dressed in his finest clothes and presented himself to the emperor and the princess. "I am the prince who sent you the rose and the bird," he told her. "I thought I loved you, but I see now that I cannot marry one who values elaborate gifts above the humble beauty of nature."

And with that, the prince set off for home.

# Sleeping Beauty

**L**ong ago, a king and queen held a grand christening for their new baby daughter. They invited twelve fairies, but left out the thirteenth, who was known for being very mean.

One by one each fairy gave the baby a gift, such as goodness, beauty and intelligence. The twelfth fairy was about to give her gift, when suddenly, in strode the thirteenth fairy. She cried, "When the princess is sixteen she shall prick her finger on a spindle and die." Then she disappeared in a flash!

The twelfth fairy spoke up quickly. "Perhaps I can soften this evil spell a little…" And her wish was that the princess would fall asleep for a hundred years instead.

Well, Briar Rose (for that was the princess's name) grew up good and clever and beautiful. Everyone loved her. But on her sixteenth birthday, she came across a little door in the castle that she had never seen before. Inside sat the thirteenth fairy, disguised as an old lady, busy at a strange wheel with some thread.

"What is this?" said Briar Rose, reaching out for the spindle. "Ouch!" she cried as it pricked her finger.

At once Briar Rose fell into a deep sleep – and so did everyone else in the palace. Years went by, and brambles grew up around the castle. Stories of the beautiful sleeping princess faded into legend.

But on the very day that one hundred years had passed, a prince came riding by. As he passed the brambles they burst into bloom. He cut his way through them and found the palace and its sleeping occupants – but he could not wake them. At last he came to the room where Briar Rose lay asleep. The prince gently kissed her and she opened her eyes.

The two walked out into the courtyard to find everyone else was waking up too! Soon, a splendid feast was held to celebrate Briar Rose's marriage to the prince, and everyone lived happily ever after.

# The Two Fellows and the Bear

**O**nce upon a time, two men were travelling through a wood together when all at once, a huge bear rushed out at them.

One man ran for his life, but the other man threw himself to the ground, face down in the dust. He kept very still, not even daring to breathe. The bear came up to him, sniffing him all over but at last it slouched off. Then, when the man who had run away saw that the bear had left, he came back laughing. "What was it the bear whispered to you?" he asked. "It told me," said the other man, "a friend who runs off and leaves you at the first sign of trouble should not be trusted."

# The Soldier and his Horse

**It was wartime,** and a soldier looked after his horse with great care. He gave it oats, and exercised it every single day, for he wished the horse to be strong.

However, when the war was over, the soldier made the horse work hard. He gave it only chaff to eat and hardly ever brushed its coat.

The time came when war broke out again. The soldier saddled his horse for battle. He loaded it with his pack and weapons, but the half-starved beast sank under the soldier's weight.

"You will have to go to battle on foot," said the horse. "Due to hard work and bad food, you have turned me into a donkey, and you cannot in a moment turn me into a horse again."

# The Glow Worm
# and the Jackdaw

**A** jackdaw swooped down on a glow worm and was about to eat him.

"Wait a moment," said the glow worm, "and I'll tell you something."

"What is it?" said the jackdaw with interest.

"There are many glow worms in this forest. If you want lots to eat, follow me."

"Certainly!" said the jackdaw.

Then the glow worm led him to a place in the wood where a fire had been lit. It pointed to the sparks flying about and said, "Look, you can see the glow worms warming themselves. Help yourself."

The jackdaw darted at the sparks and tried to swallow them, but his mouth was so badly burnt that he flew away saying, "Ah, the glow worm is a dangerous little creature!"

# The Mountains in Turmoil

**O**nce upon a time, a group of villagers built their homes around the base of some towering mountains. The mountains were like giants — huge and threatening — but the villagers didn't want to live elsewhere because the soil around the mountains was rich, and crops grew well.

One day, the earth began to quake and rocks came tumbling down the mountainside. The people were terrified that the mountains had come to life. Suddenly the earth shook violently and a gap appeared in the side of one of the mountains. The people fell to their knees and waited for the end to come.

At long last, a tiny mouse poked its head and whiskers out of the gap and came scampering towards them. 'What a lot of fuss about nothing!' thought the mouse.

# The Key to the Storehouse

**A** **rich farmer's son** was looking for a wife. He liked a local girl and went to visit her family. As he sat in their home, he saw a pile of flax. "How long does it take your daughter to spin that much flax?" he said.

"Just a day," said the mother proudly. The boy was surprised, and he slipped a key he found into the bundle. Six weeks later he visited again and pulled out the key. "Obviously a day here lasts six weeks," he said and left.

# The Gnat and the Lion

**A** **brave gnat flew up to a lion** and said, "I'm stronger than you! Let's fight." And he bit the lion on the nose.

The lion was furious, but in his haste to swat the gnat, he only succeeded in scratching his own nose. The gnat buzzed off in triumph.

However, the gnat's celebrations were short-lived. It flew straight into a spider's web, and was caught. 'No one is too great to fail,' the gnat thought sadly.

# Little Red Riding Hood

**O**nce **upon a time** there was a little girl who always wore a red riding cloak with a hood, so everyone called her Little Red Riding Hood.

One day, the girl's mother asked her to take a basket of food to her grandmother, who was poorly. Little Red Riding Hood set off through the woods.

She hadn't gone far, when she met a wolf. "Hello, little girl," the wolf said, licking his lips, "Where are you going?"

"To my grandmother's," Little Red Riding Hood replied.

That gave the wolf an idea. He ran off ahead of Little Red Riding Hood, and when he reached grandmother's cottage, he knocked on the door. But grandmother saw the wolf through the window and hid.

The wolf opened the door and, finding the cottage empty, he pulled on her nightcap and climbed into bed!

Soon Little Red Riding Hood arrived at the cottage. She found her grandmother with a nightcap pulled low and the covers drawn up over her chin, looking very odd.

"Grandmother," Little Red Riding Hood said, "what big ears you have!"

"All the better to hear you with," came the reply.

"Grandmother, what big eyes you have!"

"All the better to see you with," came the reply.

"Grandmother, what a big mouth you have!"

"All the better to eat you with!" growled the wolf. He sprang out of bed and grabbed Little Red Riding Hood. Luckily, a huntsman was passing the cottage. He took out his axe and the wolf ran out the door and away! Little Red Riding Hood and her grandmother were both safe once again.

# Raiko Captures the Monster

**In the country of Japan** there lived a brave young warrior and clever archer called Raiko. He became a palace guard at a time when the emperor was troubled by a fearsome monster. This dreadful beast had the wings of a bird, the body of a tiger, a monkey's head, a serpent's tail, and dragon's scales.

None of the guards dared to face the monster, but Raiko decided to fight the beast. He strung his bow and stood guard alone.

Towards midnight, Raiko's sharp eyes spied the beast on the roof, so he shot an arrow at it. His aim was true and down the beast fell. Raiko rushed up and captured it.

Raiko was a hero. The emperor promoted him to captain of the guard, and he carried a gold sword. To this day children in Japan tell tales of his skill and bravery.

# The Farmer and the Money-lender

There was once a farmer who suffered at the hands of a money-lender. Good harvests or bad, the farmer was always poor, and the money-lender was always rich.

One day, the farmer met a poor man sitting under a tree. Finding out he was hungry, the kind farmer gave him his last cake. The farmer told the man his troubles and the man – who was really a god in disguise – gave him a conch shell. "Whatever you wish for, blow the conch and it will be fulfilled," the god told the farmer.

The money-lender noticed the farmer's change in fortune. He kept watch on him, and when he learnt that the conch shell was the reason, he stole it. But he didn't know how to use it. So he said to the farmer, "I've got your shell, and I will give it back on one condition – whatever you get from it, I am to get double." The farmer reluctantly agreed.

From then on, no matter what the farmer gained, the money-lender got double. During a very dry season, the farmer blew his conch and got a new well – but the money-lender got two new wells! When the farmer's old

horse died, he blew on the conch and got a new horse —
but the money-lender got two new horses!

The farmer grew more and more angry. At last he could
stand it no longer. He blew on the conch
and cried, "I wish to be blind in one eye!"

The money-lender, of course, became
blind in both eyes, and in trying to find
the path between his two new wells, he
fell into one!

# New Shoes

**A**man needed some new shoes. He drew a picture of his
feet on a piece of paper, and added his measurements.
When he got to the market, he discovered that he had
forgotten the piece of paper and walked back to get it. By
the time he returned, sellers were packing up their stalls.
The man explained his situation to one of the stallkeepers.
"But how did you get to market?" asked the stallkeeper.

"I walked," said the man.

"Then you brought your feet with you," said the
stallkeeper. "Why did you need the paper?"

The man blushed, "I suppose I trusted my
measurements more than the real thing."

# The Goatherd and the Goat

**O**ne day, a goatherd was on a mountainside. It was time to take his goats to the lowlands for the night.

However, one of the goats had strayed and was refusing to join the rest. The goatherd tried to get her back by calling, but the goat took no notice. He lost his temper, picked up a stone and threw it at her. To his horror, he broke one of her horns.

The goatherd begged the goat not to tell his master, but she only replied, "My broken horn will tell what's happened, even if I keep quiet."

# Tinsel and Lightning

**A** piece of tinsel once said to a pebble, "You see how glittery bright I am! I am related to lightning."

"Indeed!" said the pebble, "How special you must be."

Sometime after, a flash of lightning struck. The tinsel was scorched by the flash and lost its brilliance.

"Where is your brilliant glitter now?" said the pebble.

"Oh," said the tinsel, "I have lent it to the lightning. It came down a moment ago to borrow it."

# The Lion and the Goat

A lion was fighting with all of the animals in a country, so a goat came up with a plan to stop it. He lay down in a cave and waited.

The lion soon found the goat's tracks, and followed them to the cave. But the goat didn't shake with fear at the sight of the lion. Instead it said, "I'm so glad you're here."

"What do you mean?" asked the lion, in surprise.

"I have eaten one hundred elephants, one hundred tigers and ninety-nine lions so far," said the goat. "I have been waiting for one more lion – you!" And he moved as if he were about to spring up.

The lion took a step backwards. 'It looks like a goat,' he thought to himself, 'but it must be a wicked spirit to have eaten all those animals.'

"Come here!" shouted the goat.

The lion turned tail and ran away as fast as he could go!

# The Clever Monkey and the Boar

Long ago in Japan, there lived a man who earned his living by taking round a monkey and showing off the animal's tricks. One evening the man came home in a bad temper. He told his wife that the monkey had grown too old to do tricks. "How will we afford food? We may have to sell the monkey to the butcher!"

His wife sighed, and said she would send for the butcher in the morning.

Now, the monkey was in the next room and he heard every word of their conversation. He said to himself, "I will go and talk to the wise boar in the forest. He'll know what to do."

So that night, the monkey slipped out of the house and told the boar what he had overheard.

The boar thought for a while and said, "I have it! Tomorrow morning I will creep into your master's house and steal their baby. Then you can rescue it from me. They will never get rid of you then!"

The next morning everything happened as planned. The husband

and wife saw the boar steal their baby — and then they saw the monkey running after the thief as hard as his legs would carry him.

Their gratitude knew no bounds when the faithful monkey brought the child safely back to their arms.

"There!" said the wife. "This is the animal you wanted to get rid of — if the monkey hadn't been here we would have lost our child forever. You will have to find another way to make money."

"You are right, wife. He will be our honoured guest from now on," said the man, as he carried the child into the house.

The couple were as good as their word, and the old monkey was very well looked after, and lived the rest of his days in peace and comfort.

# The Astronomer

There was once an astronomer who enjoyed going out to watch the stars. He liked to walk in the countryside where there was no light at all, make himself comfortable and spend hours watching the heavens.

One night, the astronomer was walking along gazing at the sky as usual. He was so absorbed with looking up that he fell into a dry well.

Luckily a passing traveller heard the astronomer's cries and helped him out of the well. Then the man asked the astronomer what had happened.

But when the astronomer explained, the traveller was not very sympathetic. "You should not look so hard at the sky that you didn't notice where your feet were going. I hope you have learnt your lesson — if we aim too high, we risk missing very important things around us."

# Soup from a Sausage Skewer

Long ago there was a lady-mouse, who told another lady-mouse about a splendid feast that had just taken place in the mouse-king's palace. "The food was wonderful! We had stale bread for starters and wax candle for the main course. Pudding was mouldy sausages. In the end there was nothing left except the skewers that the sausages had been stuck on for grilling!

"After dinner everyone started talking about an old recipe — soup made from sausage skewers. Then the mouse-king stood on an old reel of thread and said that the lady-mouse who could make the tastiest soup from a sausage skewer would be his bride. The king would give us a year and a day to find the recipe."

"Ooooh!" gasped the second lady-mouse. "How exciting!"

A year and a day later, everyone gathered at the kitchen in the mouse-king's palace. A few mice tried their recipes, but none of them tasted good. Then the smallest lady-mouse decided to try. "Will someone set the kettle on the fire? Pour the water in — quite full… now we wait until the water comes to the boil… there, I throw in my sausage skewer... and now will the mouse-king kindly dip his tail into the boiling water and stir it? The longer it is stirred, the stronger the flavour. Nothing more is needed."

"Can't someone else stir it?" asked the mouse-king nervously, looking at the boiling water.

"No," said the lady-mouse firmly. "The power is contained in your tail alone."

So the mouse-king stood close to the kettle and carefully put out his tail – closer, closer, closer... His tail had only just touched the hot steam when he sprang away from it, exclaiming, "Oh, certainly, you must be my queen! And the soup is so special that we won't make it now, we will save it for our fiftieth wedding anniversary!"

Very soon the wedding took place. But many of the mice, as they were returning home, said that the soup could not be properly called 'soup from a sausage skewer', but should be called 'soup from a mouse's tail'.

# Good Luck can Lie in a Button

There was once a man who scraped a living making umbrellas. He was so poor, he could barely afford to buy wood to make the umbrella fastenings!

One day, the wind blew down a branch from a nearby pear tree. The man carved little pears from the wood to fasten his umbrellas, instead of buttons. People loved the pear buttons so much that the man became wealthy. And from this time on the man always said: "Good luck may lie in a button."

# The Poor Man and the Angel

A poor woodcutter named Hans once met an old woman who begged him for some food. Hans had only some stew in a tin bowl — his one daily meal, but he was kind, and gave it to the stranger. The old woman ate hungrily.

Then she turned into an angel! She told Hans that because of his goodness, he would never want for anything again. From that time forth, everything went well for Hans, and he lived in comfort for many years.

# The Goose Girl at the Well

**O**ne morning, a count met an old woman in a forest. She was struggling to carry two baskets full of fruit. The count offered to carry them — and her — back to her home. The old woman was most grateful, and she jumped on this back.

When they reached the old woman's hut, an ugly girl with dull eyes and lank hair came out to meet them. The old woman explained that the girl looked after her geese.

Then the old woman gave the count a box made of a single emerald to thank him for his help. He went on his way, but was soon lost in the forest. Towards evening he reached a castle, and asked for a room for the night.

In the morning the count presented the king and queen of the castle with the emerald box, to thank them for the room. The queen opened the box and began to cry.

Through her tears she told the count, "Our daughter

was so beautiful that she cried pearls. One day she angered the king and he banished her. We have looked and looked, but never found her. Inside this box is a pearl just like the ones she cried! Where did you get it?"

The count offered to lead the king and queen to the old woman's hut. As they approached, they saw the old woman outside. The goose girl was washing her face by the well. But she looked different — beautiful! Her eyes were like stars.

The king and queen knew she was their daughter at once, and told her how sorry they were.

"Your daughter has a pure heart — yet you threw her out," the old woman scolded them. "She has lived here with me in disguise ever since."

The king said he would spend the rest of his days making it up to his daughter, and they all lived happily ever after.

# The Frogs who Wanted a King

**O**nce upon a time, a group of frogs lived in a swamp and spent their days splashing about, without a care in the world. Some weren't happy though — they thought that they should have a leader. So they prayed to the great god Zeus. "Mighty Zeus," they cried, "please send a king to rule us!"

Zeus knew the frogs were fine as they were, so he sent them a log. But the frogs prayed to Zeus again: "Please send us a king — a real king who will really rule over us."

So Zeus sent a big stork, which soon gobbled up most of the frogs. The few frogs that were left wished they hadn't asked for a king in the first place! "No rule is better than cruel rule," they croaked.

# Anansi and his Wife

**A**nansi the tricksy spider had a wife who loved to eat lots of food. Anansi was greedy and hated to share, so he asked God to give him a wife with no mouth upon her face. The next day, the new wife arrived. Her face had eyes and a nose, but no mouth. Anansi was delighted when his wife cooked a delicious meal and he ate all of it himself.

But the next day, Anansi realized lots of food was missing. Who could be eating it? He peeped in at the kitchen and saw his wife lift up her arm and poke food into a mouth in her armpit. The mouth ate and ate. Anansi went back to God to complain. "You prayed for a wife with no mouth on her face," said God. "And that's what I gave you."

# The Lark and her Young Ones

In early springtime one year, a lark made her nest in the stalks of some young wheat. She laid a clutch of tiny eggs and looked after her chicks tenderly once they had hatched.

One day, the owner of the field came to look over his crop, which was now fully grown and ripe. "The wheat is ready," he said. "I must ask my neighbours to help me with the harvest."

One of the young larks heard his words and told his mother. "Don't worry, my son," she urged. "He's not going to do anything straight away."

And it was indeed a few days before the owner came back again. By this time, though, the wheat was over-ripe. "I must come myself tomorrow with my men," said the owner.

The mother lark heard these words herself and said, "Now it is time to be off, for the man is in earnest — he no longer relies on his friends, and will reap the field himself."

# How the Lame Man and the Blind Man Helped Each Other

**T**wo men were invited to a feast at the king's palace. One was blind, while the other could not walk. "What a pity it is," said the blind man, "that we cannot go, for the food at the palace is sure to be delicious!"

"I have an idea," said the lame man. "You carry me, and I'll tell you the way to go." So the blind man took the lame man on his back and followed the lame man's directions to the palace, and both enjoyed the king's feast after all!

# The Stolen Axe

**A** woodcutter went out to cut some firewood, and discovered that his axe was missing. He couldn't find it anywhere! He saw his neighbour's son standing near the woodshed and thought, 'Aha! That boy must have stolen my axe. Look at the guilty look on his face.'

A few days later the woodcutter found his axe under a pile of firewood. "I remember," he said, "It's where I left it! Silly me!"

# Goldilocks and
# the Three Bears

**O**nce upon a time there was a girl called Goldilocks. One morning she came across a cottage. As the door was open, she went inside. On the table were three bowls of porridge – a big one, a middle-sized one and a little one. Goldilocks tasted them all. The big bowl was too cold, the middle-sized bowl was too hot. The little one was just right, so she ate it all.

By the fire were three chairs. Goldilocks sat in each of them.

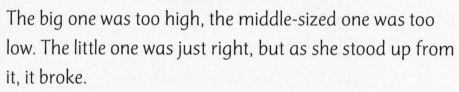

The big one was too high, the middle-sized one was too low. The little one was just right, but as she stood up from it, it broke.

Next, she went upstairs and found three beds – a big one, a middle-sized one and a little one. The big bed was too hard. The middle-sized one was too soft. The little one was just right, and Goldilocks was soon fast asleep.

Now, the cottage belonged to three bears, and as soon as they arrived home they knew that someone had been inside. Father Bear growled, "Someone has been eating my porridge."

Mother Bear grumbled, "Someone has been eating my porridge."

And Baby Bear gasped, "Someone has been eating my porridge – and it's all gone!"

Next, Father Bear growled, "Someone has been sitting in my chair."

Mother Bear grumbled, "Someone has been sitting in my chair."

And Baby Bear gasped, "Someone has been sitting in my chair, and has broken it!"

Then the bears went upstairs. Father Bear growled, "Someone has been sleeping in my bed."

Mother Bear grumbled, "Someone has been sleeping in my bed."

And Baby Bear gasped, "Someone has been sleeping in my bed – and they're still there!"

At that, Goldilocks woke up with a start! She ran down the stairs, and out of the door. And she didn't stop running until she was back in her own house.

# The Fortune Teller

**T**here was once a man who sat in the town square and told fortunes. People loved to hear what was going to happen in their future – even if it was bad news – so he was kept busy every day.

One morning, however, a boy suddenly pushed through the crowds and shouted that the fortune teller's house had been broken into by thieves. They had made off with everything they could lay their hands on! The fortune teller jumped up at once and rushed off, cursing the thieves.

A bystander chuckled to himself and said, "Our friend claims to know what is going to happen to others, but he's not clever enough to see what's in store for himself."

# The Country Fellow
# and the River

**A** **country boy** was sent to market by his mother to sell butter and cheese, but on his way he came to a fast-flowing river. The boy laid himself down on the bank to wait until the water ran out so that he could cross without getting wet.

He waited all day long but it was no good — the water would not stop! Around midnight, he gave up and went home, taking all his market goods back with him. "What's this?" said his mother. "You haven't sold a thing!"

"Well Mother, I came across a river that ran all day long, so I sat waiting for it to run out — but it is still running!"

"My son," said the woman, "The river will run forever and a day. You will never sell your butter and cheese if you wait for that!"

# Foundling

**A**huntsman was walking in the woods when he came across a baby boy. The huntsman called him Foundling, and brought him up as his own child, along with his daughter, Lina. The two were very happy together until one day, Lina heard their cook, who was a witch, planning take Foundling away.

Lina told Foundling that they had to run away — but the witch chased after them. When they heard her footsteps, Foundling changed himself into a rose bush and Lina became a rose upon it. The witch ran past but when they changed back she came after them again. This time Foundling turned himself into a pond and Lina became a duck upon it. The witch stopped at the pond to take a drink. As she leaned over the water, the duck seized her hair and tugged her into the water! The old witch sank to the bottom of the pond and the children escaped.

# The Shepherdess and the Chimney sweep

**T**here was once a sitting room in which there stood a wooden cupboard, decorated with beautiful carvings. On the middle shelf was a little man with a long beard, two tiny horns and legs like a goat. The children of the house called him Billy Goat's-legs.

On a table nearby stood a little china shepherdess. At her side stood a chimney sweep, also made of china. He and the shepherdess were in love.

Another china figure stood on the table – an old Chinaman who could nod his head. He acted as the shepherdess's father, always telling her what to do.

One day, Billy Goat's-legs asked if the little shepherdess would marry him. The Chinaman nodded his head, but the shepherdess said to the chimney sweep, "I won't marry him. I don't want to. Let's run away."

They climbed down to the floor, but Billy Goat's-legs noticed them escaping. "They are getting away!" he shouted, and the Chinaman started to chase them.

"Quick, up the chimney!" said the chimney sweep. Up and up and up they climbed, and at long last they were out on the roof.

The sight of all the houses stretching to the horizon was too much for the shepherdess. "I never dreamt that the world was so huge," she cried. "Please, take me back."

So the couple climbed back down the chimney and saw the Chinaman lying on the floor with his head broken off! He had fallen off the table as he chased them.

"Don't worry," said the chimney sweep, "he can be glued back together." And they climbed up the table and stood in their old places.

The very next day, the Chinaman was fixed and put back next to them as good as new, except he could no longer nod his head. So later on, when Billy Goat's-legs called out again, asking for the shepherdess's hand in marriage, the Chinaman did not nod in agreement. And so the little shepherdess and the chimney sweep lived happily ever after.

# The Eagle and the Kite

**A**n eagle and a kite were perched in the branches of a tree together. The eagle was very sad because he couldn't find a mate, so the kite said to him, "Why not take me? I would be a good match. In fact, I am much stronger than you. I have often carried away a fully grown ostrich in my talons."

The eagle was impressed by these words and agreed to the match. Then, one day the eagle said to his new wife, "Why don't you fly off and bring me back an ostrich?"

The kite soared into the air, but when she returned, all she brought back was a straggly mouse. "Is this," said the eagle, "the fulfilment of your promise to me?"

The kite replied, "In order to obtain your royal hand in marriage, there is nothing that I would not have promised."

# Which was the King?

King Henry of France was hunting in a forest one day. Towards evening he told his men to ride home along the road while he took a different route. As the king rode along he saw a child.

"Boy," said the king, "are you looking for your father?"

"No, sir," answered the boy. "I am looking for the king. They say he is in the woods, and may ride out this way."

"Oh, if that is what you wish," said King Henry, "get up behind me on my horse and I'll take you to see him."

The boy got up at once, and sat behind the king. "They say that the king always has a number of men with him," said the boy, "how will I know which one is King Henry?"

"That will be easy," was the answer. "All the other men will take off their hats, but the king will keep his on."

Soon they came to the main road where the king's men were waiting. They seemed amused when they saw the boy, and as the horse rode by, they greeted the king by taking off their hats.

"Well, my boy," said King Henry, "who do you think is the king?"

"I don't know," answered the boy, "but it must be either you or me, for we both have our hats on."

# The Sea-hare

There was a princess who lived in a tower. It had twelve windows, through which she could see every bit of her kingdom — so nothing could be kept secret from her.

The princess declared she would only marry a man who could hide where she couldn't find him. She thought this was an impossible task, and many men failed.

Then one day, a young man begged her to let him have three tries. As she liked the look of him, she said yes.

The young man went hunting and thought about how to hide. He was about to shoot a raven, when it cried, "I'll help you if you spare me." The young man agreed.

Next, he aimed at a fish, but it cried, "I'll help you if you spare me." The young man agreed.

Then he aimed at a fox — but it cried, "I'll help you if you spare me." The fox too went free.

The next day the man had to hide from the princess. He asked the raven for help. The raven took an egg and shut the young man inside. But the princess saw the egg move.

The day after, it was the turn of the fish. It swallowed the man, and swam to the bottom of the lake, but the princess saw the bulge in the fish's stomach.

On the third day, the fox changed the man into a small slug-like creature called a sea-hare. The fox told the young man to creep into the tower and hide under the princess's hair when she went to the window. So when the princess looked, she could not see the man.

As soon as the princess admitted she was beaten the fox returned the youth to his true form. The princess married the young man, and the two were very happy together. And the young man made sure that the raven, the fish and the fox were always well cared for.

## Saving the Bell

The foolish men of Gotham heard that invaders were coming to attack, so they decided to hide their precious church bell. They rowed to the middle of the pond and pushed the bell overboard.

"How will we be able to find it again?" they wondered.

"That's easy," one of them said. "All we have to do is mark where we dropped it in!"

So they took a knife and carved a mark in the side of their boat. They rowed back to the shore, pleased that they would be able to find their bell by the mark on the boat.

# The Cheeses that Ran Away

One day a man from Gotham filled a sack with cheese and set off to market. When he sat down to rest, a cheese slipped out of the sack and rolled all the way down the hill.

"Ah!" said the man, "So you can run to market, can you? Well, if you can go to market alone, so can the others."

So he emptied his bag, and as the cheeses rolled away he shouted, "Meet me at the market place!"

Most of the cheeses ended up in the bushes, but the man went cheerfully to the market, thinking he would meet them there. Of course the cheeses were nowhere to be seen. "I did think they were running too fast. Maybe they went too far," mused the man.

# The Fox and the Tiger

**A** **young tiger was out hunting one day** when he came across a fox. He was just about to pounce on it when the fox said, "Tiger, you must not think that you are really king of the beasts. Follow me along the road and see what happens — if people aren't frightened when they see me, then you may swallow me in one gulp."

The tiger smiled, and said he was willing to do as the fox said, so they walked along a highway where there were lots of travellers. When the people saw the tiger in the distance, they screamed and ran away. "Ah ha!" The crafty fox said, "Everyone is scared of me! You should be too."

So the tiger turned and ran, never realizing that the people had been wary of him all along.

# The Jackdaw and the Doves

One day a jackdaw noticed some doves living in a warm, safe dovecote, and saw that they were given food each day by their owner. He wished for an easy life too, so he painted himself white and asked the doves to let him in.

The doves were fooled by his disguise, and agreed that he could live with them. The jackdaw was silent, so he wouldn't give himself away by his harsh cry. However, one day he forgot himself and began to chatter. The doves kicked him out at once.

The jackdaw flew back to his own kind — but because he was white, his friends failed to recognize him and they too turned him away. So in trying to win favour with two sets of birds, he ended up gaining neither.

# Five Peas in a Pod

There were once five peas growing in a pod. The pod grew and grew, until one day – *crack!* The five peas rolled out into a boy's palm. He wanted them for his peashooter. Four of the peas landed in bushes, but one landed in a mossy crack under the attic window of a little house and took root.

A poor woman and her daughter lived there. The daughter was very ill, and they had lost hope of her recovering. When spring came, the mother opened the curtains one morning and the girl cried, "What is that green thing peeping in at the window?"

"Oh!" said her mother. "A pea has taken root and is growing green leaves. Now you have your own garden."

The woman drew her daughter's bed closer to the window, so she could see the plant. The next day the daughter said, "Mother, the little pea is growing so well, I feel I too will get better soon."

This made the woman very happy. She carefully tied a piece of string for the pea tendrils to climb as they grew.

The sick girl watched the plant growing bigger every day. She even began to manage to sit up. And it was this show of strength that made the woman believe that her sick daughter would one day be well again.

# Anansi and the Turtle

Anansi the spider had just baked some yams when Turtle knocked at the door. Anansi didn't want to share his yams, so as Turtle sat down he said, "Turtle, your hands are dirty! Please wash them."

Turtle crawled to the river to wash, and Anansi ate half of the yams. When Turtle returned and went to sit down again, Anansi said, "Your hands are still dirty! Go and wash them again!" Poor Turtle did as he was asked, and by the time he returned there wasn't a single yam left!

# Hop-toads and Pearls

A bad-tempered widow had a grumpy daughter and a kind stepdaughter, who was made to do all the chores alone, and fetch the water from a distant well.

One day when the kind girl had filled her bucket, an old woman asked for a drink. The stepdaughter helped her take a drink from the bucket. The old woman was really a fairy, and she said, "I will give you a gift to equal your goodness."

When the girl went home, her stepmother scolded her for being late. "I'm sorry," the girl replied, and as she spoke two pearls dropped from her lips.

When the girl told what had happened the stepmother called to her daughter, "Fetch water from the well, and if anyone asks you for a drink, make sure you give it!"

The eldest daughter did as she was told. The same old woman asked for a drink. The girl agreed, but she did not help her. The fairy said, "I will make you a gift to equal your rudeness."

The girl returned home, and her mother asked what had happened. But when the daughter spoke, two toads sprang from her mouth!

# The Nail

**A**fter a good day's business, a man was about to set out for home on his horse, when a stable boy said to him, "Sir, a nail is missing in the shoe on the left hind foot."

"Leave it," replied the man, "I am in a hurry."

He rode off but his horse soon began to limp, then stumble, and finally the beast fell down. The man had to continue on foot. When he was still five miles from home, robbers stole all his money. He didn't reach his house until late. "And all this misfortune," he said to himself, "is owing to the lack of a nail. Next time, more care, less speed!"

# Reynard Steals Fish

One day Reynard the fox saw a man driving a cart full of fish, and he was so hungry the sight made his mouth water. He lay down in the road, and played dead.

When the driver saw him there, he said, "That fox will make a beautiful fur scarf."

He stopped the cart, threw Reynard into the cart with the fish, and drove on.

Quick as a flash, Reynard threw all the fish out of the cart. Then he jumped out himself, and enjoyed the best meal he had in weeks.

The man didn't notice this, and drove all the way home. When he arrived at the door he called to his wife, "Ann, come and see — I got something extra for you!"

But when his wife looked into the cart she said, "Well, you seem to have brought me nothing — not even a fish!"

# The Caged Bird and the Bat

A **caged bird** longed for the skies she could see through the bars, and even though she no longer had the joy of flying, she sang with the most beautiful voice — but she sang at night, when everyone was asleep.

One night, a bat clung to the bars of the cage, and asked the bird why she sang only at night.

"I have a good reason," said the bird. "It was when I was singing in the daytime that a birdcatcher heard my voice, and caught me. Since then I have only sung at night."

But the bat replied, "It is no use doing that now, when you are a prisoner. If only you had done so before you were caught, you might still be free."

# Jack and the Beanstalk

**J**ack and his mother were very poor, so they decided to sell their only cow at the market. On the way, Jack met a little man who offered him five magic beans in exchange for his cow. Jack agreed, and ran back home to his mother. She was so cross that he had no money to show for his morning that she flung the beans out of the window.

But the next day Jack awoke to find an enormous beanstalk growing where the beans had fallen. Without any hesitation Jack began to climb it. When he reached the top he came to a vast castle, so he knocked at the door.

It was opened by a huge woman, who said, "My husband eats boys, so you'd better hide." Jack hid in a cupboard just as a giant man came into the kitchen.

"Fee fi fo fum! I smell the blood of an Englishman!" he roared.

"Don't be silly, dear," said the giant's wife. The giant then emptied a bag of gold coins onto the table, counted them, put them back in the bag, and fell asleep. At once Jack darted out of the cupboard, grabbed the bag of gold, and climbed down the beanstalk as fast as he could. His mother bought two cows with the money.

After a while Jack wanted to climb the beanstalk again.

The giant's wife was not pleased to see him. "My husband lost a bag of gold when you were here," she muttered, and then the ground began to shake. Jack hid in the cupboard again as the giant stomped in.

"Fee fi fo fum! I smell the blood of an Englishman!" he roared.

"Don't be silly, dear," said the giant's wife. The giant then lifted a golden hen onto the table, and the hen laid a golden egg. With a smile on his face the giant fell asleep. Jack darted out of the cupboard, grabbed the golden hen and climbed quickly down the beanstalk.

Jack's mother bought a herd of cows with the eggs that the hen laid in a week, and they were very happy. Then Jack decided to climb the beanstalk one last time. This time he hid under the table just as the giant entered the kitchen. "Fee fi fo fum! I smell the blood of an Englishman!"

"Look in the cupboard," said the giant's wife, but it was empty. The giant took out a golden harp, and said, "Play!"

The harp played so sweetly that the giant was soon fast asleep. Jack crept out from under the table and grabbed it, but the harp called out, "Master!"

The giant awoke and chased Jack, who scrambled down the beanstalk with the harp. As soon as Jack reached the ground, he grabbed an axe and chopped through the beanstalk so the giant could not get down. Jack and his mother lived happily for the rest of their days.

# The Little Folks' Presents

Long ago, two men were travelling when they heard music. They followed the sound and found tiny people dancing. As the men approached, a tiny man leapt up and shaved their heads! Then he told them to help themselves to a pile of coal as they left. To the travellers' amazement, the next morning, their hair had grown back and the coal had turned to lumps of pure gold.

One of the men wanted more gold so he went back. The tiny man shaved his head, and this time he filled two sacks with coal. But when he awoke the next day all his gold had vanished – and he was still bald!

# How the Camel got his Hump

**I**n the beginning, when the world was so new-and-all, and the animals were just beginning to work, there was a camel that lived in the middle of a howling desert. He refused to help with anything, and when anybody spoke to him, he just said, "Humph!"

The horse, the dog and the ox all came to him and said, "Come and work like the rest of us."

"Humph!" said the camel.

At the end of the day, the man called the horse and the dog and the ox together, and said, "Friends, I'm sorry but that humph-thing won't work, so you will have to do extra."

That made the three animals very angry (with the world being so new-and-all).

Presently the genie in charge of All Deserts, came rolling along in a cloud of dust.

"Genie," said the horse, "is it right for anyone to be idle, and not work?"

"Certainly not," said the genie. So they told him about the camel.

"Very good," said the genie. "I'll humph *him* if you will kindly wait a minute." And he went to find the camel in the middle of the howling desert.

"You've given the others extra work ever since Monday morning," said the genie to the camel.

"Humph!" said the camel.

"I wouldn't say that again if I were you," said the genie. But the camel said "Humph!" once more. Straightaway his back began puffing up into a great big lolloping humph!

"Do you see that?" said the genie. "That's your very own humph that you've brought upon yourself. You will be able to work now for three days without eating, because you can live on your humph."

And from that day to this the camel has worn a humph (we call it a 'hump' now) — but he still hasn't learned how to behave.

# The Foolish Shepherd

There once was a foolish boy who took a job as a shepherd. Everyone said he was too stupid for the work, but the farmer said anyone could guard sheep. "All you have to do," he said, "is watch the herd, and if a wolf comes, pick up a big stone like this," he picked up a stone to show him, "then throw it to scare away the wolf. Do you understand?"

The boy said he did and just a few hours later, a wolf did appear. The boy looked at the stones on the ground, but there wasn't one just like the stone the farmer had shown him! He ran back to the farm to get one and by the time he came back the flock was scattered!

After that the farmer admitted that even shepherds need some brains.

# The Donkey Carrying the Statue

Long ago in a far-off city there was a procession to the temple of an important goddess. At the front, a statue of the goddess was carried on the back of a donkey. Priests and priestesses followed, and behind them were hundreds of slaves chanting prayers and throwing rose petals.

As the donkey walked along, crowds of people bowed low in front of the statue he carried. The foolish donkey thought the people were bowing their heads to him. He puffed out his chest, threw his head back and stood still so that everyone could admire him properly.

At once the driver gave him a sharp tap with the whip, shouting, "You idiot! Do you think the people are here for you? It is not wise to take credit for the greatness of others."

# Work Hard and Do Well

A boy called Abdul grew up believing that you can do anything if you work hard enough. One day, after he saw the princess of his kingdom in her carriage, he went to the palace to ask for her hand in marriage.

The whole court laughed at the thought of a simple village boy marrying their princess. But the Caliph spoke kindly to the boy and declared, "Ages ago a ruby of great value was lost in the Tigris. He who finds it shall have the hand of my daughter."

Abdul was pleased to hear this and went to the shores of the Tigris. Every morning, he worked to drain the river so he could search its bed. The fishes in the river at last became fearful that he might take all their water away, and they came before their king to ask for his help.

"Why is he doing this?' asked the fish king.

"He wants the ruby that lies buried at the bottom of the Tigris," was the reply.

"I advise you," said the fish king, "to give it to him. For if he is determined to find it, he will work until he has drained the last drop of water."

So the next day, the fishes threw the ruby into Abdul's bucket, and he took it to the Caliph. The Caliph kept his promise and agreed that the princess could be Abdul's wife.

# The Spirit in the Bottle

A poor woodcutter and his son were working hard in the forest one day when the boy found an old bottle. Inside was a strange creature. "Let me out!" it cried.

The boy drew the cork out of the bottle, and the creature emerged, swelling until it became a mighty spirit. The spirit presented the boy with a sticking plaster. "Here is your reward for releasing me," it boomed. "One end of the plaster will heal any wound. The other end will change steel into silver." With that, the spirit vanished.

The woodcutter was thrilled by his son's good fortune. By turning steel into silver they could afford to send the boy to school. And because the boy could heal all wounds with the magic plaster, he became the most famous doctor in the whole world.

# The Farmer and the Fox

There was once a farmer who was bothered by a fox. It came into his farmyard every night, and each morning, the farmer awoke to find yet more of his chickens missing. So the farmer trapped the fox. Then he tied a bunch of dry brushwood to the its tail and set fire to it.

But in trying to escape the fire, the terrified creature ran straight into the farmer's corn fields, which quickly burnt, destroying the farmer's harvest. Revenge can be a double-edged sword.

# The Flower Princess

One morning a princess was changed into a flower by a wicked fairy. The fairy told the princess's husband the right flower in the field and picked it, she would change back into his wife. But if he picked the wrong one she would stay a flower forever.

Her husband looked closely at every flower. At last he picked a cornflower. All at once his wife stood before him.

"How could you tell it was me?" she asked.

"The other flowers had stood in the field all night so they had dew on them," he replied, "while you alone had none."

# The Donkey and the Mule

**O**ne day a man who owned a donkey and a mule loaded them up and set off on a long journey.

The donkey found it hard going. On the verge of collapse, he begged the mule to carry part of his load – but the mule refused. At last, the donkey could take no more. He stumbled and crumpled on the ground. The owner now had the problem of how to carry on with his journey. At last, he did the only thing possible – he piled the donkey's load on top of the mule's.

The mule could only just manage the extra weight, and, as it staggered painfully along, it said, "I have got what I deserve – if I had only helped the donkey, I would just be carrying half of his load."

# Cap o' Rushes

**O**ne morning a rich gentleman decided to ask his daughter how much she loved him.

"I love you as much as fresh meat loves salt," she said.

"What a silly answer – you don't love me at all!" her father said. Then he banished her from the house.

The girl made herself a hooded cloak out of some rushes to cover her fine clothes. Then she walked until she came to a palace, where she got a job as a maid. She didn't tell them her name so they called her 'Cap o' Rushes', after her reed cloak.

After a short while, it was announced that a dance was to be held at the palace, and the servants were to be invited. Cap o' Rushes said that she was too tired to go, but when the others had left she took off her reed cloak and went to the dance in her finery. The prince danced with no one else all evening and even gave her a ring as a token of his affection.

The next day the prince tried to find the girl he had danced with, but no one knew who she was. He grew so lovesick that he had to stay in bed, and was miserable.

When Cap o' Rushes heard how much the prince missed her, she made him some soup and slipped the ring into it. The prince drank it, and when he saw the ring he exclaimed, "Send me whoever made this soup!"

Cap o' Rushes was sent to the prince. He recognized her at once, and asked her to marry him.

Wedding invitations were sent to all the noble folk who lived nearby — even Cap o' Rushes' father. Cap o' Rushes asked for her father's food to be served without salt, and it tasted so bland that he realized how much she loved him. Cap o' Rushes forgave her father for his silliness, and they all lived happily ever after.

# The Boy and the Filberts

One morning a boy noticed a jar of nuts, or filberts, on a shelf. They looked so tasty that he couldn't resist reaching up and lifting it down. He thrust his hand inside the jar, and greedily grasped as many as he could hold.

But he couldn't get his hand out of the jar, for the neck was too small to allow such a large handful to get through.

Just as he burst into tears, a neighbour passed by and saw what the trouble was. "There, there," she said. "Don't be greedy. If you can be content with half of what you have, you'll be able to get your hand out easily enough."

# The Toad

A family of toads lived at the bottom of a deep, dark well. They were very content – except for the youngest toad, who felt a terrible longing to go and explore the outside world. So one day he climbed out of the well and hopped down the road into a garden.

There he met a stork who told him about the countries she had visited – especially the warm land of Egypt, where she went in winter. It sounded very exciting.

"I must get to Egypt!" the little toad said to himself. And off he hopped to see as much of the world as he could...

I do not know what happened to the little toad. But I do know the longing to explore and learn shone most brightly within him, so I wouldn't be surprised to learn that he did make it to Egypt.

# Simple Hans and the Slap

Simple Hans was in the market place when a man mistook him for someone else and slapped him. Hans reported the man to the judge and demanded that he be punished.

The judge and the man turned out to be old friends. Laughing, the judge told the man to pay Hans just one penny for the slap. The man chuckled and went on his way – without even paying that.

Hans was furious. He went back to the judge and asked, "Are you telling me the fine for a slap is one penny?"

When the judge said yes, Hans slapped the judge on the face, and said, "You may have my penny when your friend comes back with it."

# A Wild Goose

**T**wo men went out to hunt geese and soon they saw a fine one fly overhead. One man fitted an arrow to his bow and said, "I'm going to enjoy that goose roasted with sage and onions!"

"Sage and onions!" exclaimed the other, "NO! Apple sauce and green peas is the only way to cook goose."

"Sage!" insisted the other.

"Apple!"

"Sage!"

"Apple!"

"Right," said the man, "Let's ask our village headman."

The village headman was very wise and declared the goose should be cooked half one way and half the other. The men were content with this and went back to fire the arrow... but of course the goose was long gone.

# The Princess and the Raven

A king was lost in a forest one evening. As he wandered, he came across a great raven. The raven offered to guide the king home, on the condition that he could marry the king's daughter.

Reluctantly the king agreed, and the raven led him out of the forest. But when they reached the castle, the king thought he could trick the raven, and sent it away with his shepherd's daughter instead.

The raven took the girl back to his nest, and offered her a drink in a golden goblet, a silver cup, or an earthenware jug. The girl chose the jug, so the raven knew he had been tricked.

So the king sent his steward's daughter. The raven offered her the three drinks. This girl chose the white wine, so the raven knew he had been tricked again.

Now the raven was angry. He threatened to summon all the birds and tear down the castle. At this, the king sent the raven his daughter – the true princess. The raven offered her the drinks and she chose the golden goblet.

At once the raven changed into a handsome prince. "At last I am free!" he said. "I was under a spell that could only be broken when a real princess drank from the golden goblet."

# The Owl and the Birds

**A**n owl once advised **the rest of the birds** that whenever they noticed a little shoot growing from an acorn, they should pull it up out of the ground.

"Why should we?" asked the lazy birds.

The owl told them that acorns encouraged mistletoe to grow, which humans used to make sticky bird-lime. Then hunters would paste the bird-lime onto reeds. The sticky reeds would be placed in trees, bushes and hedgerows. And then the birds would get stuck to the reeds and be caught by the hunters.

The birds all thought the owl had gone mad, and took no notice of her. But the owl was right, and many of birds were caught in traps just as she described. They learnt too late that owls are the wisest of birds.

Now, when any owl is asked for her advice, she no longer gives it — because it was once so ignored.

# The Sun and the Moon

In the beginning the Sun and the Moon quarrelled. The Sun said, "You are only the Moon and are not much good. If I did not give you light, you would be no good."

But the Moon answered, "You are only the Sun, and you are very hot. The women like me better, for when I shine at night, they go outdoors and spin."

The Sun was so angry it threw sand in the Moon's face – and you can still see the dark spots on the Moon today.

# The Beggar's Dream

Once upon a time there was a poor beggar who was very thin and hungry. One day, a friend asked him why he looked so sad.

"I had a dream that I was invited to the palace of the king. The walls were hung with silk and the cushions stuffed with down. His majesty himself offered me a plate of meat. Would I have cold ham or a hot roast chicken?

I asked for the chicken. Well, the king went away to see about it being cooked and while he was gone, I woke up. And now I'm kicking myself I didn't ask for the ham."

# Arachne the Weaver

There was once a little Greek girl called Arachne who was so proud of her weaving that she boasted she could even beat the Goddess Athena at it. Her friends warned her it was dangerous to say she was better than a goddess, but she was so sure of herself she didn't stop.

One day an old woman asked her, "Do you really mean what you say?"

"Yes," Arachne replied. "My weaving beats everyone's."

In a flash the old woman disappeared and Athena stood in her place. "Let us have a competition," she said.

Arachne's weaving was very fine, but Athena's was so delicate it nearly floated away. Arachne was beaten, and as punishment Athena turned her into a spider.

"Ah well," sighed Arachne. "At lease I can spend my life weaving."

# The Windmill

A long time ago, there stood a windmill on a hill. It had been there as long as anyone could remember and looked rather as if it was growing out of the countryside.

"I am very lucky," it said to itself, "that people like looking at me. I have been here for many years. And I know that the time will arrive when I will become old and tumble down. But I will be built up again, newer and better. I will look different, but as long as I have the miller and his wife living at my heart, and the children running around me, I will be the same deep down inside. And everyone will say: 'There's the mill on the hill – what a sight to see.'"

And so the days passed, and the days came, until one afternoon the windmill caught fire and burnt down.

Very luckily, the miller's family were not at home at the time. They were filled with sadness to lose the old mill, but they soon built a beautiful new mill, even better than the first. And the miller and his wife lived at the heart of the new mill and their little children ran around it like thoughts. Its windows were always brightly lit, and its sails creaked steadily round and round while it stood there, thinking deeply. And everyone said: "There's the mill on the hill – what a sight to see."

# The Lion in Love

There was once a lion who fell in love with a girl, so he went to her parents to ask for her hand in marriage. The parents did not wish to give their daughter to the lion, yet they did not want to make him angry either.

At last the father said, "We fear that you might injure our daughter. May we suggest that you have your claws removed and your teeth pulled out. Then we will consider your proposal again."

The lion was so much in love that he did indeed have his claws cut and teeth removed. Then he went again to see the parents, with high hopes that they would agree to the marriage. But this time they just laughed in his face, for now that love had tamed him they had no reason to be afraid of him.

# The Cloud of Dust

**T**wo men wanted to raise wild boars for meat, so they went in search of some piglets. They soon found a cave that was home to a family of boars. The men hid outside and waited until the mother boar left. Then one man went into the cave to fetch the piglets while the other man kept watch outside for the mother.

All of a sudden the mother boar came charging back, tusks ready to slash. The man outside just had time to grab her tail! As the mother boar struggled to free herself, a great cloud of dust was thrown into the air.

From inside the cave came a shout, "Where has all the dust come from? I can't see!"

His friend outside shouted back, "Well, if this tail breaks, you'll find out what it means!"

# The Princess and the Pea

Long ago there was a prince who wanted to marry a true princess. He had been searching for a long time, but hadn't found anyone he liked.

Then one evening there was a knock at the palace door. A girl, claiming to be a princess, was outside in the rain. She asked for shelter for the night and the prince let her in. The queen didn't trust the girl, so she came up with a plan. She placed a pea on the girl's bed and ordered that twenty mattresses be piled on top of it. Only a true princess would feel the pea!

The next morning the queen asked the girl how she had slept. "Oh, very badly!" the girl sighed. "There was something hard in the bed, and now I am very sore." The prince — who had fallen in love with the girl as soon as he saw her — was overjoyed that she was a real princess. And so the two were married and they lived happily ever after.

# The Three Dogs

One day a shepherd set out to seek his fortune. He hadn't travelled far when he came across a man with three dogs. "Will you swap your three sheep for my three dogs?" the man asked. "The smallest one is called Salt, and will bring you food whenever you wish. The second is called Pepper, and he'll fight to protect you, and the big one is called Mustard. He can break iron with his teeth."

The shepherd thought that the dogs sounded very useful, so he swapped. Every day Salt brought him a fine meal, so the shepherd was happy.

A few days later the shepherd came across a carriage with a beautiful girl inside. The coachman told him that he was taking the girl to a dragon who lived nearby. Every year the dragon demanded a maiden to eat, and this year the king's daughter had been chosen. The shepherd decided to save the girl and when he reached the dragon's lair he called, "Pepper, help!"

The loyal dog fought bravely to protect his master and at long last he scared the dragon away.

The princess asked the shepherd to come back to her castle, but the shepherd told her that he wanted to see the world, and he would return in three years.

As soon as the shepherd was out of sight, the coachman turned to the princess and said, "Tell your father that it was I who defeated the dragon, or I'll kill you!"

The king was so relieved to have his daughter back that he offered the coachman her hand in marriage as a reward. The girl begged for the wedding to be put off, and the coachman grudgingly agreed.

After three years of waiting the coachman told the king he would delay no longer. On the same day, the shepherd returned and heard of the coachman's lie, and the marriage. He ran to the church, but guards barred the door, and when the shepherd began to shout they threw him in prison.

In despair the shepherd called, "Mustard, help!"

The dog bit through the iron prison bars, releasing him. The shepherd climbed onto Mustard's back and they raced to the church — just in time. The coachman was banished from the kingdom, and the princess and the shepherd were married at last.

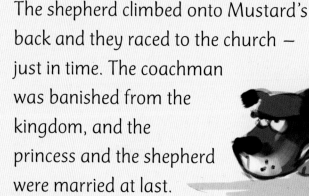

# The Farmer's Favourite Daughter

**O**nce upon a time there was a farmer with two daughters, who asked him which one of them was his favourite. "I love you both the same," was always his answer, but they did not accept this.

Finally he secretly gave them both a blue bead, telling each one that she should tell no one of the gift.

After that whenever either of the daughters asked him, "Which one of us is your favourite?" he would answer, "I love best the one to whom I gave the blue bead," and each one was satisfied with his answer.

# The Grasshoppers and the Ants

**A**ll summer the ants worked to gather food for winter, but the grasshopper did nothing but sing from dawn to dusk. When winter came, the grasshopper was very hungry. At last he had to beg the ants for some grains.

The ants asked, "Why didn't you collect a store of food?"

"I didn't have the time," replied the grasshopper. "I was too busy singing."

The ants gave him a little food. "But know for next time that it's best to be prepared," they said.

# The Norka

**M**any years ago, a king and queen lived with their three sons. One day a Norka – a monster with mighty claws and sharp, red teeth – came to the kingdom. The royal family knew that their people would not be safe until the Norka went away.

Each of the two elder brothers tried to catch the Norka, and both times it escaped and then returned. Now it was the turn of the youngest son, Prince Ivan so he set out into the forest where it had last been seen.

Suddenly, the Norka came rushing through the trees. Prince Ivan gave chase, following it down a deep, dark hole. When he crawled out of the hole he found himself in another world, deep under the earth, and the Norka was nowhere to be seen.

Prince Ivan walked until he came to a palace made of gold. He knocked at the door, and it was opened by a woman so beautiful that Prince Ivan fell in love with her at once.

Prince Ivan told the woman about the Norka. She told him that she was a princess from a faraway land. "The Norka captured me many years ago.

No one has been able to defeat it, though many have tried. It is currently asleep on a rock out in the sea. Please capture it!"

So Prince Ivan journeyed on, until he reached the shore and saw the Norka fast asleep in the middle of the sea, as the princess had described.

He reached it by hopping from rock to rock, and before the Norka realized he was there, he chopped off its mighty claws and sharp, red teeth! The Norka was so upset, it swam away, never to be seen again.

After his victory, Prince Ivan returned to the golden palace and asked the princess to marry him, and she said yes! Then they travelled back to the upper world, where they lived happily ever after.

# The Brave Tin Soldier

**O**ne Christmas, a boy was given twenty-five tin soldiers. They were all exactly alike except for one, which only had one leg. There hadn't been enough tin to finish him.

The boy started playing with his new toys, arranging them by a cardboard castle. Near the castle stood a cardboard lady. She was a dancer and one of her legs was raised so high that the tin soldier thought that she, like himself, had only one leg.

Then the boy lined the tin soldiers up on the windowsill. But the one-legged tin soldier got blown out of the window. He landed in the street below, and was soon spotted by two boys. They made a paper boat, placed the tin soldier in it, and sent him sailing down the canal. Of course, his boat began to sink, and the water closed over the brave tin soldier's head.

Next the soldier was swallowed by a fish! How dark it was inside its mouth! He waited… and waited… and finally daylight opened over him. A voice cried out, "I don't believe it, here is the missing tin soldier!" The fish had been caught, taken to the market and sold to the boy's mother. The boy was overjoyed to have his tin soldier back again.

# The Blind Man and the Cub

There was a blind man who had so fine a sense of touch that when any animal was put into his hands, he could tell exactly what it was. One day, a wolf cub was placed in his hands, and he was asked what he thought it was. He felt the cub all over, and then said, "Indeed, I am not sure whether it is a wolf's cub or a fox's, but this I do know — it would never do to trust it with a flock of sheep."

# Straw, Coal and Bean

An old woman took some beans and made a fire on which to cook them. One bean fell onto the floor where it met a piece of straw and a lump of coal. They became friends, and decided to seek their fortunes together.

They set off, and soon came to a brook. The straw laid across the brook, so the other two could walk across it.

When the coal reached the straw's middle, the straw caught fire and fell into the brook, and the coal slid in after it. On the bank, the bean laughed so hard that it burst!

Luckily, a passing tailor took some black thread and sewed the bean back together again. And that is why all beans now have a black seam.

# The Fox without a Tail

**O**nce upon a time, a fox caught his tail in a trap. He struggled and struggled to get free, and in the end he broke loose – but his tail was left behind.

The fox was embarrassed about no longer having a tail but he was determined to put a bold face upon his misfortune, and summoned all the foxes to a meeting.

When everyone had assembled, the fox proposed that all foxes should do away with their tails. He pointed out how inconvenient a tail was when they were pursued by dogs and when they wanted to sit down. "That is all very well," said one of the older foxes, "but would you be asking us to cut off our tails if you had not lost your own?"

# Mercury and the Woodman

Long ago, a woodman lost his axe in a river. The god Mercury came to help him and dived into the water. He emerged holding a golden axe.

The woodman was tempted to say the fine axe was his, but he shook his head. "That's not my axe."

Mercury dived again and recovered the real axe, which the man accepted. Mercury was so pleased with the woodman's honesty that he gave him the golden axe too!

The woodman told the story to his friends, and one of them decided to see if the same would happen to him. So he dropped his axe in the river.

Mercury appeared, dived, and brought up a golden axe. "That's mine!" the man cried.

But Mercury was so disgusted at the man's dishonesty that he flew away, taking the golden axe with him and leaving the other one in the river.

# King Solomon and the Baby

**K**ing Solomon used to judge people's arguments. One day two women came before him, both claiming that the baby they had brought with them was their own.

King Solomon thought for a while then said, "You both say the baby is yours — the simplest thing to do is cut the baby in half and give you half each. Do you agree?"

"Yes," said one woman.

But the other cried out, "No! No! Let her have it."

"Take your baby," said Solomon to the one who had said no. "You are clearly the true mother. You would give it up sooner than let it suffer harm."

# The Sphinx

**Y**ears ago in Egypt, there was a monster called the Sphinx. It had the body of a lion and the head of a woman, and it stood guard at the entrance to a shortcut through the desert. No traveller could pass her unless they answered her question correctly — and no one could!

One day a young man called Oedipus decided to try. "What animal goes on four legs in the morning, two legs at noon, and three legs in the evening?" asked the Sphinx.

Oedipus thought for a long time, and then said, "Man! In childhood he crawls on hands and knees, as a grown-up he walks on two legs, and in old age he needs a stick to help him."

At this the Sphinx uttered a cry and ran off into the valley below. Oedipus had answered correctly and people no longer travelled in fear.

# Thumbelina

OCTOBER
14

There was once a woman whose daughter never grew bigger than a thumb, so she called her Thumbelina.

They lived happily together until one night a horrid mother toad decided that Thumbelina would be the perfect wife for her son. She grabbed Thumbelina and put her upon a floating water lily leaf in the middle of a stream.

Thumbelina didn't want to marry a toad! Luckily some fish heard her cries and nibbled at the stem until the leaf was swept away.

All summer, Thumbelina lived alone in the woods. She ate honey and drank dew. When winter came and she had to search for shelter, Thumbelina met a mouse who said, "You can live with me while its cold."

One day a mole came to visit his friend the mouse. The mole was charmed by Thumbelina and invited her and the mouse to stay with him. The mouse agreed, and the three set off through underground tunnels to the mole's house. On their way they passed a sick swallow on the ground.

That night Thumbelina crept back down the tunnel with a blanket to spread over the swallow. "Thank you," he whispered.

Thumbelina looked after the swallow in secret all through winter. When spring arrived, Mr Mole asked her to marry him.

"You're lucky," the mouse told her, "he will make a splendid husband."

Thumbelina could not bear the thought of a life underground. That night she asked her friend the swallow what she should do.

"I am strong enough to fly now," he replied. "Climb on my back."

"Oh yes, please!" said Thumbelina, and they soared up and out into the bright air. The two lived together very happily in the swallow's cosy nest.

# The Olive Tree and the Fig Tree

**H**igh on a hill grew an olive tree. It taunted its neighbour, the fig tree, about how she lost her leaves every autumn. "You are bare till spring, but I am green all year."

That year winter brought heavy snow. The flakes fell harmlessly through the bare branches of the fig, but they settled on the leaves of the olive tree. The weight of the snow on the leaves was so much that some of the olive tree's branches broke. "I should not have boasted," she sighed. "For no one is too good to meet with misfortune."

# The Chattering Magpie

**T**here was once a woman who had a talking magpie. One morning her husband caught an eel. He told his wife that he would serve it to a friend for dinner. But while he was at work, his wife ate the eel herself.

When the husband came home, the magpie said, "Master, my mistress ate the eel."

The woman grabbed the magpie and pulled every feather from its head. And from then on, whenever the magpie saw a bald-headed person, it would squawk, "You too must have told about the eel!"

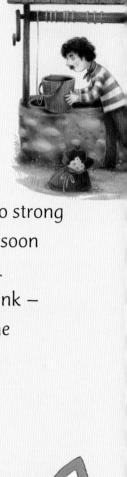

# The Cheese Thief

**O**ne afternoon, a man reached into his bag for his lunch and realized that he had been robbed. His chunk of cheese had gone!

"Go and search the roads," said his wife, "Look in the alleys and find the man eating your cheese."

But the man had a better idea. "That cheese is so strong and salty," he said, "that whoever has taken it will soon need a drink of water." So he sat by the village well.

In a short while a stranger came up to take a drink — and when the man searched his pack, there was the remains of his cheese!

# Puss in Boots

**A** miller's son inherited a cat from his father. "What am I to do with a cat?" he said. Imagine his surprise when Puss replied, "Give me some boots and a bag and you shall see!"

So the son did as Puss asked. Puss went to a field and put carrots in the bag, then he hid in the grass. Before long, a rabbit hopped into the bag, tempted by the carrots. Off Puss ran to the palace, where he offered the rabbit to the king as a gift from the Marquis of Carabas. The king was delighted.

The next day, Puss said to the miller's son, "Come to the river and help me fish." Puss knew the king would be driving by in his carriage.

"Quick, get into the water!" said Puss. The miller's son did, just as the carriage passed by. Then Puss hid his master's clothes. "STOP!" cried Puss. "My master, the Marquis of Carabas, has been robbed! Thieves stole his clothes as he swam in the river!"

The king gave the miller's son some clothes, and offered to take him home in his carriage. "It's this way, Your Majesty," said Puss, and he ran on ahead. He met some workers gathering hay in the fields. "When the king's carriage drives by, the king will ask who owns this land," said Puss. "Say it belongs to the Marquis of Carabas." Sure enough, this is what happened. The king was impressed.

Puss ran on until he came to a big castle. He asked to meet the ogre that lived there. "What do you want?" the ogre growled.

Puss said, "Is it true you can turn yourself into any animal? Can you turn into a lion?" The ogre did so with ease. "It must be easy to turn into a big animal," said Puss. "Could you turn into a mouse?"

As soon as the ogre changed into a mouse, Puss pounced on him and ate him up.

When the king's carriage arrived, Puss went outside to meet it. The king was so impressed with the castle that he offered the Marquis of Carabas his daughter's hand in marriage! Puss was very pleased at the way his plan had worked out, and the miller's son made sure Puss spent the rest of his days living in luxury.

OCTOBER
19

# The Wind and the Sun

The wind and the sun were arguing about which was the stronger of the two. "Do you see that traveller?" said the wind. "Let's try our strength on him. Whoever can strip him of his cloak will be the winner."

"Agreed," said the sun.

The wind began first. He blew a blast that made the traveller stagger. But the traveller only drew his cloak tightly around his shoulders, and kept on his way.

Then the sun tried. He beamed down upon the traveller's head and shoulders. "Ah!" cried the man, "It is so hot!" He threw off his cloak, and carried it under his arm. After that, the wind never claimed to be stronger than the sun.

# The Bat, the Bramble and the Seagull

**A** bat, a bramble, and a seagull once decided to go on a voyage together. The bat borrowed some money for the trip, the bramble brought clothes, and the seagull gathered an amount of lead. They loaded a ship and sailed away but they soon hit a great storm. The boat sank, but luckily the three travellers were washed ashore.

Ever since then, the seagull flies over the sea, every now and then diving below the surface, looking for the lead he's lost. The bat is so afraid of meeting the moneylenders he borrowed from that he only comes out at night. And the bramble catches hold of the clothes of everyone who passes by, hoping someday to recover its lost garments.

# Nasreddin Hodja
# and the Smell of Soup

A hungry beggar passed a restaurant with cauldrons of delicious soup. He was so ravenous that he couldn't help but lean over and take a deep breath. At that moment the innkeeper seized him. "You haven't paid!" he exclaimed.

"But I've had nothing," said the beggar.

"You must pay for the smell," insisted the innkeeper. The poor beggar had no money to pay, so the innkeeper dragged him off to the judge, Nasreddin Hodja.

Hodja listened to the story then said to the innkeeper, "I myself will pay you." Then he held some coins up to the innkeeper's ear and shook his hand.

"Now you may go," he said.

"But what about my payment?" spluttered the innkeeper.

"This man took the smell of the soup," said Hodja, "and you have been paid with the sound of the money. Now go on your way."

# The Red Shoes

O nce, there lived a little girl called Karen whose family couldn't afford to buy her shoes. But the shoemaker's wife felt sorry for her, so she took some leftover red leather and made her some. Karen loved them dearly.

Soon after, Karen's mother fell ill. Karen's father had to work, and couldn't look after her too. So Karen went to live with a rich old lady. She was given lovely new clothes and shoes, and people told her she was beautiful.

When the queen and princess visited the town, the old lady took Karen to see them. Karen saw that the princess had a lovely silk dress and a pair of red leather shoes. They were even prettier than the ones that the shoemaker's wife had made for Karen. The next time the old lady took Karen to buy shoes, Karen insisted on choosing a pair of red shoes just like the ones the princess had worn.

The old lady couldn't see well, so she didn't notice when Karen wore her bright red shoes to church. All the time she was meant to be saying her prayers, Karen was admiring her shiny red shoes. After the service, several people told the old lady about Karen's shoes. She was extremely cross and said Karen must wear black shoes in future.

But when the next Sunday came around, Karen put on her red shoes again. At the end of the service, an old man

was sitting outside. "What pretty dancing shoes!" he said
to Karen. "Never come off when you dance," he told the
shoes.

As she walked home, Karen couldn't resist dancing a
few steps — and once she began, she couldn't stop! She
danced away from the church and down the street… and
then all the way out of the town. All she could do was
dance, over fields and valleys, for miles and miles.

Late that night the dancing shoes finally carried Karen
right back into the church, but still she could not
stop dancing. Karen wept — she was truly
sorry for her disobedience. All at once,
the shoes stopped dancing.

Karen kept the now tattered
red shoes as a reminder of her
silliness, but she was
quite happy to never
wear them again!

# The Water of Life

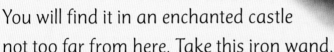

**L**ong ago, a king fell gravely ill. His son was on the verge of despair, when a dwarf appeared before him and told him, "The Water of Life will save your father. You will find it in an enchanted castle not too far from here. Take this iron wand. When you reach the castle, hit the door three times with it and it will open. Throw this bread to the lions and they will not eat you up. Then hurry in and find the well — but be quick, for when the clock strikes twelve, the castle door will shut and you will be trapped there forever."

The prince thanked the dwarf, who then showed him the road he should take. Then he vanished.

When the prince arrived at the castle, everything was as the dwarf had told him. At the third rap with the wand, the door flew open. He threw the bread to the lions and hurried past them into the depths of the castle. At last, he found the well. He drew up the bucket and poured water into a bottle, just as the clock began to strike…

*One! Two! Three!* The prince dashed back through the courtyards… *Four! Five! Six!* He sped through the castle… *Seven! Eight! Nine!* He raced past the lions. *Ten! Eleven!* He reached the castle door and leapt through. *Twelve!* He heard the heavy door clang shut behind him forever.

He jumped on his horse and set off home at a gallop. As soon as he got back he gave his father the Water of Life to drink and the king soon recovered. He arranged a splendid feast to celebrate – and of course the dwarf was the most important guest.

# The Impostor

One day a sick man prayed to the gods to help him, and promised that if he got better, he would sacrifice one hundred oxen to them.

The gods were curious to see how the man would keep this promise. So they helped him recover quickly. The man then made one hundred little oxen out of wax and offered them up to the gods. The gods were furious!

So the next night the gods sent the man a dream telling him to go to the seashore, where he would find one hundred gold coins.

When he awoke, the man hurried to the shore and dug up the coins. But a band of robbers appeared and stole the coins – all one hundred of them.

# The Lion, Jupiter and the Elephant

The lion, for all his size and strength, was afraid of the sound of a cockerel crowing. He was very embarrassed about his fear, and didn't like to talk about it. One day the lion met the elephant and they got talking. While they chatted, the lion couldn't help but notice how often the elephant flapped his ears. Then a gnat came humming by, and the elephant said, "Do you see that little buzzing insect? I'm terribly afraid that it will get into my ear."

The lion's spirits rose at once when he heard this. "For," he said to himself, "if the elephant, huge as he is, is afraid of a gnat, I needn't be so much ashamed of being afraid of a cockerel, which is ten thousand times bigger than a gnat."

# Buchettino

Once upon a time there was a boy called Buchettino. One day he found a penny and bought some figs, and went to eat them in a tree. While he was eating, an ogre passed by, and said, "My dear Buchettino, give me a little fig with your dear little hand."

Buchettino threw him one, but it fell in the dirt. Then the ogre repeated, "My dear Buchettino, please don't throw it – give me a little fig from your dear little hand!"

Poor Buchettino leant down to pass the fig, and at once the ogre grabbed him and put him in his bag.

When the ogre stopped to rest and put the bag on the ground, Buchettino cut open the bag from within. Then he filled it with large stones, and ran away.

Well, the ogre was furious when he found out, and he went looking for Buchettino in the town. At last he saw him on a balcony, laughing. The ogre nearly burst with rage, but he said, "Buchettino, how did you manage to climb up there?"

Buchettino answered, "I put dishes upon dishes, glasses upon glasses, pans upon pans – and I climbed up on them and here I am."

"Ah! Is that so?" said the ogre. Quickly he made a great mountain of kitchenware and began to climb up it. But

when he was nearly at the top everything fell
down and he crashed to the ground. He
was so cross that he went off to
another country and
never troubled
Buchettino again.

# The Emperor's New Clothes

**Years ago** there lived an emperor who loved new
clothes. One day, two men arrived who said they could
weave a cloth that only wise people could see, so the
emperor ordered an expensive suit from them.

After many days, the weavers displayed what they said
were the clothes. The emperor could see nothing, but he
dared not appear foolish. He let the men 'dress' him in
the suit and then set out on a parade. The people could
not see the clothes either, but nobody liked to say so.

Then a child's called out, "But he's naked!"
Everyone realized they'd been tricked. Highly
embarrassed, the emperor returned to his palace
to find the weavers, but they — and all the
money — were long gone.

# The Old Woman in the Wood

Once there was a servant girl who became lost in a dark forest. To her surprise, a white dove came flying up to her with a little golden key. It said, "Go to that tree over there and use this to open it."

Inside the tree, the girl found bread and milk. Then the white dove gave her a second key. "This key will open that bigger tree," it said.

The girl found a beautiful little white bed inside! She had a long sleep and felt refreshed.

"Will you do something for me?" asked the little dove.

"Of course," said the girl.

"Thank you," said the dove. "I'll lead you to a small house. Go in without speaking to the witch at the door. You will find yourself in a room filled with rings. Find the plainest one and bring it to me."

The girl did as the dove said. She didn't speak a word when the witch opened the door, but hurried past her into

the room filled with
rings. Every surface
sparkled with gold and
silver and jewels. The girl
began hunting for the plain
one and finally, tucked away
in a corner, she found it.

She took the ring and didn't
stop running until she was back in
the forest – but she couldn't see the
dove anywhere. The girl leant
against a tree to rest and
suddenly felt the branches behind
her move. As they wrapped around
her waist they became two arms!
The girl turned to find that the
tree had become a handsome
young man.

He said, "The witch cast a
spell that made me a dove
for two hours every day
and a tree for the rest of the time. By taking her enchanted
ring you have set me free!"

Then the young man and the brave, kind servant girl
lived happily ever after.

# The Snowdrop

It was **wintertime** and a bulb pushed out a little white bud on a stalk, with thick, narrow leaves. Sunbeams shone down on it. "Welcome!" they sang.

The flower was so joyful that she didn't mind when a girl picked it.

One day, the girl wrote a poem about the snowdrop, then posted it in a letter. The letter was opened by the girl's sweetheart who read it delightedly. He placed it between the pages of his favourite book.

The flower stayed within the pages of the book for years. The girl and her sweetheart were married and had a daughter. One day the daughter was looking for something to read. She reached up to a shelf and took down a book and opened it. "Why, here's a flower!" she said. "It must have been put here for a special reason! I wonder what its story is…"

# The Vain Jackdaw

Long ago, the great god Jupiter announced that he would appoint a king of the birds, to rule over them. The jackdaw realized that with his ugly plumage, he would have little chance. So he stuck the bright feathers that the other birds had dropped all over his body. But when the birds assembled before Jupiter the other birds turned on the jackdaw and stripped him of his feathers. "A fine outer appearance does not make you more special," they told him.

# The Lion, the Mouse and the Fox

A lion was once asleep when a mouse ran over his back. The mouse's feet tickled the lion and he woke with a start. He looked around to see what had disturbed him.

A fox lurking nearby saw this happen, and he thought it would be great fun to have a joke at the lion's expense.

"I've never seen a lion afraid of a mouse," said the fox.

The lion was embarrassed, but tried to pretend he wasn't. "Afraid of a mouse?" he said. "Not I! It's his bad manners I can't stand."

# Ten Jugs of Wine

It was New Year's Eve, and ten friends decided to celebrate together with a party. To make it fair they agreed that they would each bring a jug of wine to be poured into a big punch bowl. However, each person thought the same thing: "My wine is too good to share. If I bring water, no one will be able to taste the difference."

And so they gathered together on New Year's Eve and poured the contents of their jugs into the big bowl. Then they ladled out a cup for everyone – and looked guiltily at one another as water was served all round.

# St George and the Dragon

St George, the bold knight, once came to a land where a terrible dragon ate a maiden every year. This year it was the turn of the king's daughter. The people begged St George for his help, and he agreed to try to save her.

He put on his strongest armour, and with his sword in his hand, rode into the Valley of the Dragon. As soon as the dragon caught sight of the brave knight, it spread its wings and prepared to attack.

The dragon was so fierce that St George was nearly knocked to the ground. But he recovered himself and struck a mighty blow with his spear. This made the dragon furious! It hit him so violently with its tail that St George fell from his horse. Purely by chance, he landed under the shade of a flowering orange tree, the scent of which had such power that no beast dare come within its branches – so the dragon could not strike!

When St George's strength returned, he rose and struck the dragon on its belly. A deadly poison poured out, which burnt away the St George's armour, but he came forward again, and struck the dragon under one of its wings. The dragon fell to the ground, dead. Victorious, St George rode to the palace where the king's daughter washed and bandaged the weary knight's wounds. Then he lay down to rest, while she lulled him to sleep with her golden lute.

# The Miser and his Gold

**A** **very greedy man** once loved to hoard his money. He grew worried that it might be stolen so he put it in a chest and buried it in his garden.

Every night, the man would dig up the chest, count his coins, then bury his treasure once more. One night, however, a robber saw him dig the chest up. He waited until the man had gone back inside, then dug up the chest and stole it. When the greedy man discovered the theft he wailed until his neighbours came.

He told them how he used to count all his gold.

"Did you ever spend any of it?" asked one neighbour.

"No," said the man.

"Then in future come and look at the hole," said a neighbour, "it will do you just as much good."

# Everyone is Right

**N**asreddin Hodja was serving as a judge when a man complained against one of his neighbours. Hodja listened to the man then concluded, "Yes, you are indeed in the right." Then he listened to the other man's defence before pronouncing, "Yes, you are quite right." Hodja's wife turned to him and said, "Husband, the men do not agree with each other so both men cannot be right." Hodja simply answered, "Yes, dear wife, you are quite right."

# The Ants

**L**ong ago, ants were people and made their living by farming the land. But they were always looking longingly at their neighbours' crops, which seemed much better than their own. Whenever they could lay their hands on their neighbours' produce, they stole it.

When Jupiter saw how badly the people were behaving, he was so furious that he changed them into ants! Although their bodies changed, their nature remained the same, so to this day, ants go about the cornfields and gather the fruits of others' labours — and store them up for their own use.

# Dick Whittington and his Cat

**H**undreds of years ago there lived a poor orphan boy called Dick Whittington, whose only possession was a cat. One day they travelled to London and when they arrived, Dick looked around in astonishment. There were so many people and buildings! Before long, he was hopelessly lost. He stumbled into a doorway, and fell fast asleep.

The house belonged to a rich merchant called Mr Fitzwarren. He took Dick and his cat in and gave Dick a job in his kitchen. Dick worked hard, and everyone liked him.

Now, whenever one of Mr Fitzwarren's ships went to sea, he asked everyone in the household to give something to the ship's cargo for luck. Dick had only his cat, so he handed her over.

The ship was at sea for many months before it came to port in China. The crew went ashore to show the emperor the cargo, but to the emperor's embarrassment, the feast that had been prepared for the visitors was ruined by rats.

The captain smiled, "I think I have the answer." He sent for Dick's cat, and within minutes, there were piles of dead rats. The emperor was so pleased that he gave the captain a ship full of gold.

Back in London, Dick had decided to return home, but he had not gone far when he heard the church bells ringing. They seemed to say,

*"Turn again Whittington,*

*Thrice Lord Mayor of London."*

Dick decided to stay in the city, and when the ships came home, Mr Fitzwarren gave Dick his share of the gold, and more. This was the start of Dick's prosperity. He went on to become Lord Mayor of London three times. He never forgot his early poverty, founding hospitals and schools for the poor. And there were always lots of cats in his house as well!

# The Heat of a Candle

**M**ula bet his friends that he could survive a night on an icy mountain with nothing whatsoever to keep him warm. He set out to win his bet, taking only a book and a candle. Mula shivered all through the night but when he came down, his friends asked, "Did you take anything with you?"

"No," said Mula, "just a book and a small candle to read by."

"What!" they said, "Then you had some heat – you lose!"

A week later Mula invited his friends to dinner. They waited for hours for the food to be ready. "I'm sorry dinner is taking a long time," said Mula, "Come and see why!"

In the kitchen there was a huge pot of water under which a small candle was burning. Mula said, "I've been trying to heat this pot of water over this candle since yesterday and it's not warm yet!"

# The Seven Ravens

**T**here was once a widow who had seven sons and one daughter. The daughter was sweet and good-natured, but the boys were loud and wild. One day, when they were causing trouble, the widow cried, "I wish you would all turn into ravens!" The next second, her sons had vanished and seven ravens flew out of the window.

Their little sister was so upset that she decided to set out into the wide world to find her brothers, taking nothing with her but a little ring.

She journeyed till she came to the sun, but it looked much too hot and fiery. Next she ran away to the moon, but the moon was cold and chilly. So she travelled on and came to the stars, and they were friendly and kind to her. The morning star gave her a little bone, and said, "With this you can unlock the glass mountain, and there your brothers live."

The little girl travelled on until she came to the glass mountain, and she used the bone to unlock the door. Inside she found a table set with seven little plates and glasses. She took a drink from each glass and let the ring fall into the last one.

Suddenly she heard a fluttering in the air, and she hid behind the door. Seven ravens appeared and looked for their little plates and glasses. Then said one after the other, "Who has eaten from my little plate? And who has been drinking out of my little glass?"

When the seventh came to the bottom of his glass, he said, "Has our little sister come? If so we shall be free!" When the little girl heard this, she ran forward, and in an instant all her brothers took their true form again. They hugged and kissed each other, and went merrily home.

# The Brother and Sister

There once lived a couple who had a good-looking son, and a plain daughter. To save conflict, the children's parents made sure that they never saw their reflections.

This worked well, and the children played happily together. But one day, they found their mother's mirror. The boy saw how handsome he was, and began to boast to his sister. Hearing this, the father told his son, "Make good use of what you have learnt. Try to be as kind as you are handsome, or risk losing the true beauty that lies in the sweetness of your nature."

# The Dog, the Rooster and the Fox

A dog and a rooster became great friends and agreed to go on a journey together. They travelled all day, and at dusk found a tree that looked like a good place to sleep. The rooster flew up into the branches, and the dog curled up inside the hollow tree trunk.

At dawn the rooster awoke and began to crow. Hearing this, a hungry fox came and stood under the tree and begged him to come down. "I should like," said the fox, "to get to know one who has such a beautiful voice."

The rooster wasn't fooled. He replied, "Wake my butler who sleeps at the foot of the tree. He'll let you in." So the fox rapped on the trunk, out rushed the dog — and the fox had to flee!

# The Little Horse and its Kind Master

**T**here was once a foolish man who laid a heavy sack of wheat across his horse's back, while he sat behind it. He had not gone far when another man said, "That's a heavy load. Why do you not walk and lead your horse?"

"I can't," replied the first man, "My foot is lame."

"Then you should take the bag on your shoulder," said the other, "So the horse won't have to carry that, too."

"All right," said the first man, and he hoisted up the bag.

"Ah," said he, when he got to market, "My horse looks exhausted. Thank goodness I was able to help him."

# Robert and the Fairies

Robert Roberts was a carpenter who worked very hard indeed. One day, a little man came up to him and said, "Robert Roberts, go to the holly tree on the hill, dig below it, and you'll be rewarded."

Next morning, Robert Roberts did as he was told and he found a box of gold. He returned every week, and found gold each time!

One day Robert Roberts told someone who he wanted to impress that he was friends with the fairies. A week later when he went back for more gold as usual, big stones came rolling down the hill! Robert Roberts had to run for his life, and he never went near the place again. Fairies don't like people who tell about them.

# The Golden Goose

**O**nce upon a time there was a man who had a son called Duffer. Everyone thought Duffer was a fool and laughed at him.

One day, Duffer went into the forest to chop wood. He was hacking away at a tree when a little man came up and asked him for food and drink. Duffer shared his food and when they had finished the little man said, "Chop down that tree over there and you will find something precious." Duffer did so, and to his great surprise, he found a goose with feathers made of gold sitting in the roots. He picked her up carefully and went to an inn for the night.

That night, the innkeeper's daughter crept into Duffer's room to look at the goose. She tiptoed over to it and stroked the wing. But her hand got stuck to it! No matter how much she pulled, she couldn't let go.

Not long afterwards, her sister came creeping in. She too reached out to stroke the golden goose and got stuck! Then a third sister came and the same thing happened to her.

In the morning Duffer picked up the bird and strolled out with the three girls hanging onto it. Soon, they met a vicar who grabbed the youngest girl's hand to pull her away. But as soon as he touched her, he was stuck too!

Before long a farmer came by. He touched the vicar's sleeve — and that was that!

"Hey!" called the farmer to two farm workers. "Come and help me!" But soon they were firmly attached as well! Now there were seven people running behind Duffer and the goose.

Soon they came to a city where there was a princess who never laughed. The king had announced that whoever could make her laugh could marry her. The minute the princess saw Duffer and his golden goose, with all the people stuck fast behind them, she burst out laughing!

The king was delighted, and the royal wedding took place at once, with much celebrating and rejoicing.

# The Rooster
# and the Pearl

A proud rooster was strutting up and down the farmyard among the hens one morning when he suddenly spied something shining in the straw. "Aha!" said the rooster. "Whatever it is, it's for me."

He looked all around to check that no one was watching him, then he scratched and pecked and rooted the object out from beneath the straw. It turned out to be a pearl that had somehow been lost in the yard.

Although it was clearly very beautiful, the rooster was mightily disappointed. "To humans, you may be a treasure," he sighed. "But I would much rather have a single barley seed to eat than a whole string of pearls, for they are of no use to me."

# The Pied Piper of Hamelin

The town of Hamelin had become plagued with rats and its people were in despair. They had almost lost hope when one day, a strange man appeared. He promised to rid the town of the pests for a fee, and the town council agreed. So he put a pipe to his lips and when he played all the rats followed him. He led them to the river where they all drowned.

But when the piper asked for his money, the council refused. With a grim smile, the piper put the pipe to his lips again. This time all the children followed wherever he piped. He led them far away and the townspeople never saw the children again.

# The Silver Coin

Lots of coins were being made at a mint when a silver coin came out very excited, shouting, "Hooray! Now I am going out into the wide world."

And so it did. The coin was used by many people to pay for things before he was given to a man who was about to travel to many different countries. The traveller decided to keep the silver coin with him for good luck.

But one day, the coin slipped out of the man's pocket! It was found by a woman, but when she tried to use it, the shopkeeper pointed out to her that it was from a different country, and he wouldn't accept it.

The poor silver coin realized that, so far from home, it couldn't be used as money at all. The woman kept it, but a man stole it from her and then sneaked it in with some other coins to buy a lottery ticket.

The coin continued to be passed from person to person – always slipped in with other coins to make it less noticeable – until one day it was passed back to the same traveller who had brought it from home. A smile spread over his face and he said, "A coin from my own country. How strange that it's somehow come into my hands. It must be lucky!"

# Belling the Cat

Long ago, a group of mice were terrorized by a cat.

The mice held a meeting to discuss how they could outwit their enemy. Some said this, and some said that, but at last a young mouse got up and said, "You will all agree that our danger lies in the sly way in which the enemy lurks about, waiting for us. If we could receive some signal of her approach, we could easily escape. I therefore propose that we get a small bell and attach it round the neck of the cat. Then we will always know where she is and when she is coming."

This proposal met with a lot of clapping, until an old mouse got up and said, "But who is going to volunteer to tie the bell on the cat? It is easy to think of impossible solutions."

# The Wolf in Sheep's Clothing

There was once a wolf who kept trying to steal sheep from a flock. The shepherd and sheepdogs were very watchful and always chased the wolf away, but the wolf did not give up. He hung around, waiting for a chance.

An opportunity came one day when he found a sheepskin that had been cast aside. He put it over his coat and tied it around him, so he was quite disguised. Then he strolled among the sheep — none of them noticed anything strange. In fact, the lamb of the sheep whose skin the wolf was wearing began to follow the wolf.

The wolf led the lamb away from the flock and made a meal of her. And so both the shepherd and the sheep learnt the hard way that appearances can be deceiving.

# Snow-white and Rose-red

A **poor widow** lived with her two daughters, Snow-white and Rose-red. The girls did everything together and promised never to leave each other.

One freezing winter's night there was a knock at the door. It was a big, black bear! The bear said, "Please don't be frightened — all I want is to warm up in front of your fire."

Snow-white and Rose-red took pity on the bear and let him in. He was very well behaved, and soon they were quite comfortable with him. They even brushed the snow from his shaggy fur.

The next night the bear arrived at the same time in the evening, and again spent the night by the fire. And so it went all winter, with the bear knocking at their door at the same time each evening.

Then one day, spring arrived. That morning, the bear said, "Now I must go away."

"But where will you go, dear bear?" asked Snow-white.

"Into the forest, to guard it from dwarfs."

The girls were sad, but the bear promised to return next winter.

A week later, the sisters went into the forest to fetch

firewood. Near a fallen tree, they saw a dwarf, who had got the end of his long beard caught in the tree trunk. Snow-white cut off the end of the beard, freeing him. "You've cut off a piece of my beard!" the dwarf cried, most ungratefully as he ran off.

The next week, the girl's mother sent them to town to buy needles. On the way they saw an eagle seize the very same dwarf and attempt to carry him off. The girls grabbed hold of the little man and pulled against the eagle so hard that at last it let go and flew off.

"You've ripped my coat to pieces!" the dwarf yelled. "I'll curse you!" Just as he began to mutter a spell, there was a loud growl and a huge bear came out of the forest. He knocked down the dwarf with one swipe of his paw.

The girls stood trembling. But the bear said, "Do not be afraid." And at once they recognized their friend. Then the bear transformed into a handsome man, dressed in gold.

"I am a prince," he said, "and I was bewitched by that dwarf. At long last he is gone and the spell is broken."

Everyone was full of joy. Snow-white married the prince and Rose-red married his brother. And they all lived happily together for many years.

# The Dancing Gang

**A**girl once went to the river to fetch some water. When she dipped her pot into the water she caught a crayfish. But the crayfish began beating his claws on the pot, and played such a beautiful tune that the girl began dancing.

When the girl did not come back, another girl went to look for her. But when she heard the tune, she too began to dance. Person after person went to find them, until the whole village was dancing! Only when one wise girl tipped the crayfish back into the water could everyone stop.

# The Farmer and the Boggart

**O**nce upon a time a man grew some wheat in a field. He was preparing to reap the wheat when a boggart burst out of the earth. "This is my field!" it shrieked.

The farmer suggested that whoever could reap the most wheat in the morning should have the field, and the boggart agreed. But that night the farmer placed iron rods on the boggart's side. In the morning the farmer cut lots of wheat, but the boggart threw down its scythe in anger.

"This wheat is impossible to cut! You have the field!" it cried. With that it vanished and was never seen again.

# The Boy Bathing

**A** boy once fancied bathing in the river, as it was a hot day and the water looked so fresh and cool. He wasn't a very good swimmer, but he stripped off his clothes and stepped into the water.

He began jumping about and splashing — until suddenly the riverbed dropped away from him and his feet could no longer touch the ground. He was out of his depth and in danger of drowning.

Fortunately, a man who was passing heard his cries for help. He went to the riverside and began to scold him for being so careless as to get into deep water. "Oh, sir," cried the boy, "please help me first and tell me off afterwards."

# The Teapot

Once there was a proud teapot made of fine china. She would talk to anyone who would listen about her long spout and graceful handle. She boasted about her delicate design all the time and would never let anyone forget it.

"The people could drink their tea out of glasses or bowls, so the teacups aren't of that much value. But without me — why, no one could drink tea at all!"

Now the cream jug, sugar bowl and teacups were tired of hearing the teapot talk in this way — especially when they knew her lid was cracked and chipped!

Then one day, the person pouring out the tea dropped the teapot! She fell to the floor, her spout broke in half and her handle snapped off. Once the other members of the tea set had got over the shock, they burst out laughing!

The people cleared the mess away. They filled the broken teapot with earth and planted a flower bulb in it. The teapot was pleased, for now she had a heart. "I have never had a living heart until now," she said to herself. "I must be even more important than ever."

And the cream jug, sugar bowl and cups and saucers welcomed a brand new teapot on to the tea table, who was modest and polite and fitted into the tea set very well.

# The Lion and the Statue

**O**nce upon a time, a man and a lion were travelling companions on a long journey. In the course of conversation they began to boast about how strong and bold they were, each claiming to be more courageous than the other.

And so they went on, squabbling all the way, until they came to a crossroads where there was a statue of a man overpowering a lion.

"There!" said the man triumphantly. "Look at that. Doesn't that prove that men are stronger than lions?"

"Not so fast, my friend," said the lion, "that is only your view of the contest. If lions could make statues, you may be sure that you would see the man underneath."

# Nasreddin Hodja's Recipe

**N**asreddin Hodja bought a piece of meat at the market, and on his way home he met a friend. Seeing the meat in Nasreddin's hand, the friend told him a recipe for stew.

Nasreddin wrote down the recipe, and continued on his way, the piece of meat in one hand and the recipe in the other. He had not walked far when a hawk swooped down, snatched the meat, and flew away with it.

"It won't do you any good!" shouted Nasreddin after the disappearing hawk. "I still have the recipe!"

# The Honeybee's Sting

**Z**eus, the king of Mount Olympus, said he would give each animal, bird or insect a gift to help them through their life. Some chose to be able to run fast, some to have thick scales to protect them, some to have stripes or patterns to disguise them. To Zeus' surprise, the honeybee said, "I'd like the power to inflict pain whenever I choose."

"What a cruel wish!" said Zeus, "I will grant it because I promised I would. But you will have to choose when you use this gift because using it will cost you your life."

And to this day, the little honeybee dies after it stings.

# The Little Red Hen
# and the Wheat

One day a little red hen found a grain of wheat in the barnyard, and said, "Who will plant this wheat?"

"I won't," said the dog.

"I won't," said the cat.

"I won't," said the goose.

"I won't," said the turkey.

"I will, then," said the little red hen. So she did. The wheat grew until it had a big head of ripe grain at the top.

"Who will reap this wheat?" said the little red hen.

"I won't," said the dog, the cat, the goose and the turkey.

"I will, then," said the little red hen and she did.

Then she said, "Who will thresh this wheat?"

"I won't," said the dog, the cat, the goose and the turkey.

"I will, then," said the little red hen and she did.

"Who will take this wheat to the mill to have it ground?" said the little red hen.

"I won't," said the dog, the cat, the goose and the turkey.

"I will, then,"

said the little red hen. So she took the wheat to the mill, and she came back with the flour.

"Who will bake this flour?" said the little red hen.

"I won't," said the dog, the cat, the goose and the turkey.

"I will, then," said the little red hen. So she baked the flour and made a loaf of bread.

"Who will eat this bread?" said the little red hen.

"I will," said the dog, the cat, the goose and the turkey.

"No, I will," said the little red hen — and she ate the loaf of bread all up.

# The Spider and the Fly

Mr Spider wanted to marry Miss Fly. Many times he told her of his love and begged her to become his wife, but she always refused, for she did not like him.

One day when she saw Mr Spider coming, Miss Fly closed all her doors and windows and got a pot of hot water. When Mr Spider called, she answered by throwing hot water at him. This made Mr Spider angry and he cried, "I will never forgive you for this! My descendants and I will never give you any peace."

Mr Spider kept his word, and even today you can see how much spiders hate flies.

# Rumpelstiltskin

**O**ne day a miller told a lie to make his family seem more important. "My daughter knows how to spin straw into gold!" he boasted.

The news spread to the king, who ordered the girl to be brought to his palace. To her horror, the king showed her to a room piled with straw and ordered her to spin it into gold by morning. Then he locked her in.

But as the girl started to cry, a little man appeared and said he would help her if she would give him her first-born child. The miller's daughter was so desperate that she agreed. The little man sat down and bundle after bundle of straw was spun into gold.

The next morning the king

could not believe his eyes. He was so impressed that he decided to marry the miller's daughter the very next day.

They were very happy together, and a year later she gave birth to a son. Her happiness was complete — until the little man suddenly appeared. "Give me what you promised," he demanded.

The queen offered him everything else she had but he refused. At last he agreed that if she could guess his name he would let her off. He would give her three days to find it out. Then he vanished. The queen thought frantically of every name she had ever heard and sent out messengers to search for other names, but two days went by and she knew in her heart that they had not yet found the right one.

Late on the last evening a messenger returned and said, "Many miles from here I came across a little man dancing in the woods. He was singing, 'No one can guess that Rumpelstiltskin is my name!'"

When the little man appeared that night to claim the child the queen said to him, "Is there any chance that you could be called… Rumpelstiltskin?"

"WHO TOLD YOU?" roared the little man. He jumped up and down so hard that the ground beneath his feet split open and swallowed him up — and he was never ever seen again.

# How the Moon and Stars Came to Be

**O**ne day in the times when the sky was close to the ground, a young girl went out to pound rice. Before she began her work, she took off the beads from around her neck and the curved comb from her hair, and hung them on the sky, which at that time hung low all around her like blue coral.

Then she began working, and each time she raised her pestle into the air it hit the sky. For some time she pounded the rice, and then she raised the pestle so high that it struck the sky very hard.

Immediately the sky shot up into the air so far that she lost her beads and comb. They never did come down — the curved comb became the moon and the beads are now the stars that we see scattered about.

# The Wolf and the Kid

Goats are very good at scrambling up and down steep mountainsides and can often climb where others can't go.

Once day a young goat climbed onto the roof of a farmyard shed and looked down proudly on everyone below. Just then, a wolf slunk by, casting his eyes around greedily for a meal.

The kid began to tease the wolf — for he felt quite safe up on the roof.

"Mr Wolf, you are a thief. I don't know how you dare show your face near the homes of honest folk. We know the crimes you commit!"

"Curse away, my young friend," said the wolf. "You know that I can't reach you at this very moment. It is easy to be brave when you are a safe distance from danger."

# The Inchcape Rock

In the depths of the North Sea lies the Inchcape Rock. It has wrecked many ships and is a danger to those who roam the water. To warn sailors of the dangers nearby, the holy Abbot of Aberbrothock put a bell next to the rock.

But a wicked sailor called Ralph the Rover hated the Abbot, and one day he decided to sink the bell to spite him.

Just a few weeks later Ralph was very sorry that he had done so, when his own boat hit the Inchcape Rock, and sank with all onboard. For none of the sailors could hear the Abbot's bell ringing when it lay at the bottom of the sea.

# The Thistle's Tale

Long ago, a rich family once lived in a large manor house with a beautiful garden.

One day the family had visitors from abroad. The weather was fine, so they entertained their guests in the garden. Someone suggested that the girls should look for their favourite flower, so that one of the men could pick it for them.

One pretty girl from Scotland, however, couldn't find a flower she liked until she neared the fence by the roadside. There she saw a large thistle – the flower of Scotland, and she asked the son of the house to pick it for her. After he handed it to her she threaded it through his buttonhole.

The young man was delighted – and so was the thistle bush. "I must be something very special!" it said. "I suppose I should really be inside the garden, not outside the fence. Well, I've managed to get one of my lovely flower children inside at least!"

A few days went by and then a little bird told the thistle bush that the lovely Scottish girl had agreed to marry the son of the house. "And all because of me!" exclaimed the thistle bush. "Now surely someone will dig me up, take me into the garden and replant me there."

But the thistle bush remained where it had always been. The summer and autumn went by. Then one day, a thought struck the thistle and it said to itself, "Maybe if you are a parent, and good things happen to your children, you don't mind if good things don't happen to you."

# The Fir Tree and the Bramble

There was once a forest in which there lived a very proud fir tree. She thought she was better than all the other trees because she grew taller and straighter than any other plants around her.

One day she boasted to a bramble in a very snooty manner. "You poor thing, you are of no use whatsoever. Now, look at me – I am useful for lots of things. When people build houses, they always choose fir. They can't do without me."

The bramble wasn't upset. "Ah, that's all very well," she replied, "but you wait until people come with axes to cut you down. Then you'll wish you were a bramble and not a fir."

# Where are the Kittens?

The children came in with their mother from the garden and found the cat sitting in her basket, mewing sadly. Where were her kittens?

"Oh, Mummy," said Alice, "Something is wrong! Look, there's things all over the floor and the kittens are missing. Do you think a fox might have carried them off?"

"I hope not," said Mummy, looking worried. "It does look as if something big has been in here – look at that basket on the floor, and all those papers."

They started to tidy up when suddenly Mark gave a shout. He had picked up the basket and there, underneath it, were the three kittens.

"I found the kittens," said Mark, "and I think I found who made the mess too!"

# The Three Sillies

One evening, a gentleman went to visit the girl he was courting at her parents' home. The girl went to the cellar to fetch beer, and noticed an axe stuck in a ceiling beam. "Suppose once I'm married, I have a son, and he grows up, comes down here and the axe falls on his head!" she said. The thought was so sad that she sat and cried.

After a while her mother went to see why she was taking so long. She found her daughter crying and beer pouring all over the floor! "What is the matter?" said her mother.

The girl told her mother her sad thought. Her mother thought it was sad too, so they both sat and cried together.

Then the father began to wonder why they hadn't returned, so he went down to the cellar. "What is the matter?" he said.

"Why," said the mother, "look at that axe." And she told the tale. At this, the father sat down and started crying too.

The gentleman grew tired of waiting by himself, and he went to see what they were doing. He found all three sitting and crying, with beer all over the floor around them. The gentleman asked, "What is the matter?"

When the father told him the sad thought the gentleman burst out laughing. "I've never met such sillies as you three," he said as he reached up and pulled out the axe.

# The Robe of Nasreddin Hodja

Nasreddin Hodja, bruised and limping, met one of his neighbours at the market place.

"My friend, what has happened?" asked the neighbour.

Hodja answered, "Last night my wife grew angry and kicked my robe down the stairs."

"But how could that have caused your injuries?" asked the neighbour, confused.

"I was wearing it at the time," explained Nasreddin, with a frown.

# The King and the Puzzle

One day the Queen of Sheba visited King Soloman with a puzzle to test his wisdom.

She held up a bunch of flowers in each hand. "One of these," said the queen, "is made of flowers from your garden. The other is made of artificial flowers. Which is which?"

Thoughtfully, the king said, "Open the window!" A bee flew to the flowers in the queen's right hand. "The bees have given you my answer," said Solomon. And the queen said, "King Solomon you are indeed very wise."

# The Lion's Share

A lion once went hunting with a fox, a jackal and a wolf. Working together, they caught a stag — then discussed how they would share it out.

The lion demanded that they divide it into quarters. "The first quarter is for me," he declared, "because I am King of the Beasts. The second quarter is mine, because I'm sorting out the shares. The third share is mine because I helped hunt the stag. As for the fourth quarter, well, I'd like to see which of you will dare to lay a paw upon it!" And the lion bared his teeth and flexed his claws furiously. The other three hunters realized they had little hope of getting a mouthful, and slunk away into the shadows.

# Grandma's Christmas Gifts

**G**randma Burns sat knitting one morning. It was nearly Christmas, and the snow lay deep on the ground. She heard little sobs outside her door and found Peter and Jimmy Rice crying.

"What can be the matter?" asked Grandma.

"We haven't any money for sleds!" sighed Jimmy.

"Why, boys can't have a good time without sleds," said Grandma, cheerily. "Let us see if we can't find something."

Grandma found a tray and a large metal pot, and sent the happy boys away. All that day she knitted faster than ever — for she was planning something now. That evening, she went to see the carpenter. He promised to make two small sleds in return for the pair of socks she was knitting.

On the night before Christmas she tied the sleds to Peter and Jimmy's door, and then went home, smiling all the way.

# The Fox and the Little Red Hen

**O**nce **upon a time** there was a little red hen. She lived near a fox and his mother.

One day the fox sneaked into the hen's house and hid behind the door. When the little red hen came in and saw the fox, she flew up to a peg on the wall.

"Ha, ha!" laughed the fox, "I'll soon get you down," and he began running round and round after his tail.

The little red hen watched him, and she soon grew so dizzy she fell off the peg! The fox put her in his bag, and started for home, but he soon grew tired and sat down to rest. Then the little red hen tore a hole in the bag, and crept out. She found several large stones, put them in the bag in her place, and ran off home.

After a while the fox got up and carried on his journey. "How heavy this little hen is!" he said to himself. "She must be very plump and fat."

When the fox arrived home his mother called, "Have you got the little red hen?"

The fox emptied his bag in triumph – and then hopped in pain as a stone landed on his foot. Never again did they try to catch the little red hen.

# The Horse of Brass

**A** **knight arrived** at the palace of King Cambuscan, the noblest king in the East, riding a brass horse.

"The king of India," the knight said, "has sent you this horse. It can take you anywhere in the world."

"Tell me how to work it," said the king delightedly.

"To ride, remove this peg and name the place you wish to go. To stop, turn this wooden pin. If you turn this iron pin, he will vanish. He'll return when you call his name."

The knight left, and the king approached the horse. He turned the iron pin and the horse vanished. But only then did King Cambuscan remember that the knight had not told him the horse's name!

So if you ever learn the name of the brass horse you should go to King Cambuscan's palace and shout it — I'm sure it will appear.

# The Precious Stove

One day poor Peter's family had to sell their gold and white stove. It was their only precious possession. When men arrived with a cart to take the stove away, Peter hid inside it. Many miles later the cart stopped moving, and Peter poked his head out of the top of the stove. Who should he find looking at him but the king!

When the king heard Peter's story, he said, "Although I can't return the stove, I will give you the job of looking after it, and I will send money to your parents."

So the stove continued to be precious to Peter's family.

# The Spartan's Answer

The people of Sparta in Greece, were famous for their simple way of life, their skill in battle and their habit of never saying more than they needed to. Near them was a land called Macedon, and this land was ruled by a king named Philip, who wanted to rule all of Greece.

Philip sent a letter to the Spartans and said, "Surrender now, for if I enter your country, I will take everything."

When Philip received te Spartans' answer, he found only one word written there. That word was "IF."

# The Crab and the Fox

There was once a crab who lived in a rock pool at the seashore. He was happy for a time, but soon grew bored and restless, seeing the same surroundings all the time. The crab wanted a change of scenery, so he left the beach and went inland, scurrying sideways.

There, he found a meadow, which looked beautiful – lush and green, and filled with flowers. He settled there, hoping it would be a good place to live.

But then a hungry fox came along. The fox had never seen a crab before, and thought he smelled delicious! The crab could not easily escape – there were no rocky hiding holes in the meadow like there were in his rock pool.

Sure that he would be eaten, the crab sighed to himself, "I should have been content with what I had."

# The Pot that would not Walk

One day, a man who was known for being silly was getting ready to go to the market. "Husband, we need a new iron pot for the fireplace," said the man's wife.

So the man did his shopping and bought a pot. He placed it on his shoulders and started for home, but it was very heavy. He soon grew tired and set it down.

While he was resting, he noticed that the pot had three legs. "What a pity I didn't see those legs before!" cried the man. "You have three legs and I have only two, and yet I have been carrying you. That doesn't seem fair. Well, you shall take me the rest of the way, at least."

So the man climbed into the pot and said, "Go on – I am ready." But the pot stood still on its three legs.

"Ah!" said the man, "you are stubborn! You want me to carry you, but I shan't. I'll tell you the way, and you can stay where you are until you are ready to follow me."

So he told the pot where he lived and how to get there, and then off he went. When he reached home his wife asked him where the pot was and the man explained. His wife was much more sensible than he was and hurried off to get the pot. When she brought it home the man said, "I am glad you have fetched it – it might have walked back to the market if we had left it alone much longer."

# The Lion and the Mouse

Once, a little **mouse** was caught by a big, hungry lion. "Please let me go," cried the mouse, trembling in terror, "and I shall never forget you. I may even be able to help you one day." The lion was amused at the thought of the mouse being able to help him, so he let him go.

Sometime after, the lion was caught in a trap. Hunters bound the lion and tethered him to a tree while they went to get a wagon to carry him away. Just then, the little mouse happened to pass by, and he recognized the lion at once. It took the mouse just moments to gnaw away the ropes, and the lion was free.

"You see?" said the mouse. "Was I not right after all?"

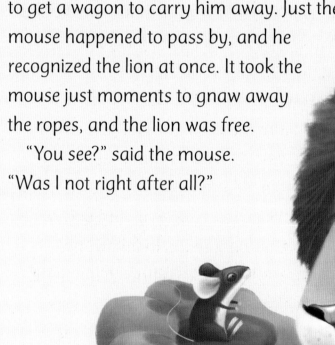

# The Fox and the Crow

**A** **hungry crow** saw a piece of cheese on the ground, so she grabbed it in her beak and flew into a tree to eat it.

A fox was lurking in some bushes nearby, and licked his lips at the thought of the cheese. He strolled up to the foot of the tree and cried, "Mistress Crow, I'm sure you have a beautiful voice. Sing for me, please, so I can tell everyone that you are the Queen of Birds."

The crow was thrilled by this praise. She lifted her head and began to caw – and the cheese fell to the ground, just as the fox had planned. The fox pounced on it at once and ate it all up, and the crow learnt never to trust flatterers.

# The Birds in the Wheat Field

**T** **he men of Gotham** once hired a man to scare away the birds from their wheat field. Unfortunately, the man had big feet and a lot of the grain was trampled.

The men came up with a plan. They got an old gate, had the man sit on it, and they carried him through the wheat fields as he scared the birds away. "He will not trample any more of our grain with his big feet now," said the silly men of Gotham.

# The Smuggler

One day a clever smuggler led his donkey to a border between two countries. The official at the border was suspicious — he thought the man may have something valuable concealed in the donkey's heavy load of straw. He searched and searched, but found nothing. "I'm certain you're smuggling something," the official said, as the man crossed through. Each day for ten years the same man came to the border with a donkey. Although the official checked the straw bundles everytime, he could never find anything.

Many years later, after the official had retired, he happened to meet that same smuggler in a marketplace and said, "Please tell me, I beg you. What were you smuggling?"

"Ah," said the man. "I was smuggling donkeys."

# Who was the Luckiest?

**O**nce upon a time, a rose bush stood blooming beautifully in a garden. A woman whose elderly mother had recently passed away came into the garden. She picked a rosebud and took it to place on her grave. The rosebud trembled with joy. "I am the luckiest flower."

Soon, another woman came into the garden. She took the largest rose, and put it in a bowl to make sweet-smelling potpourri.

"What an honour," sighed the rose. "I am the luckiest."

Then, two young men came strolling along. One was a painter and the other was a poet. Each of them picked a lovely rose. The painter created a picture of his flower. "This rose will live on, while all the others fade and die," said the painter. The poet decided to write a poem about his rose, and said, "A painting will fade one day, but a poem can live in people's minds forever." So every rose had its own story. And every rose was sure that it was the luckiest one.

"I am very lucky too," said the wind, "I know the story of all the roses and I can spread it throughout the world. Perhaps it is I who am the luckiest of all."

# The Man with the Coconuts

**A** man and his horse were once heading home after a long day of gathering coconuts. The man asked a boy at the roadside how long it would take him to get to the next town, as he was feeling very tired. The boy saw that the man's horse had a basket on either side, both of which were full of coconuts. "If you go slowly," said the boy, "you will arrive very soon, but if you go fast, it will take you all day."

The man didn't understand, so he hurried his horse. But the coconuts bounced out of the baskets and he had to stop to pick them up. He climbed back into the saddle and hurried his horse to make up for lost time, but the coconuts fell out again. On the third try he let his horse walk slowly. The coconuts stayed in the baskets, and he understood what the boy had meant.

# One's Own Children
# are always Prettiest

A man once went into a wood where he met a curious little bird – a snipe.

"Please spare my children," said the snipe, "You'll know them because they are the prettiest birds in all the wood."

The man agreed, but then the snipe saw him walking home, and her children had been caught. "I caught the ugliest birds I could find!" the man protested.

The snipe sighed, "Don't you know that everyone thinks their own children are the prettiest?"

# The Goat and the Vine

A goat wandered into a vineyard one day and found vines hanging heavily with juicy grapes. The goat began to graze on the tender green shoots. Then it heard a voice. The vine was speaking!

"Eat as much as you want – I will still make wine to add to the pot when you are being cooked as a stew."

The startled goat stopped grazing and trotted away at once.

# The Legend of the Christmas Rose

**A** **robber woman** lived deep in the forest with her five wild children. When she needed more food than they could catch themselves, she begged from the townsfolk, who feared her and would not let her live among them.

One day, the robber woman promised to show the townsfolk a magic garden if they would forgive her wild ways. They agreed, and at midnight she took them to the forest. All was dark, but then a beautiful garden appeared, with many flowers blooming together, their scent heavy in the air.

The townspeople cried that it was bad magic, and the garden faded from their sight. Only a single white root remained. This was gathered by a small boy. The townspeople planted it and on Christmas Eve it blossomed. It had silver leaves and flowers, and was the first Christmas rose.

# The Swan and the Raven

A raven once caught sight of a swan and couldn't help but feel jealous of the elegant bird's long neck and snow-white feathers. The raven became eaten up with envy – all he could think of was how he too could get the same beautiful plumage!

'Maybe the swan's clean colour comes from the water in which he swims?' the raven wondered. So he went to soak himself in the swan's lakes and pools. But no matter how many times the raven washed, he didn't become even a tiny bit white. Instead, he was bedraggled and hungry, as he couldn't find any food.

In the end, he returned to his old home and had to be satisfied with his lot.

# The Snail and the Butterfly

**A** snail once thought to itself, 'I wish I was a butterfly', as it watched a beautiful peacock butterfly flitting by. The snail slid slowly across the grass, looking for tender shoots to eat, and envied the butterfly's delicately painted wings.

Just as the snail reached a tall plant, the skies darkened and huge drops of rain began to fall heavily. The poor butterfly darted under the plant and hung there shivering and terrified.

"If the rain hits my wings, it will damage them," it said. "If only I could be somewhere safe and dry."

"I wish I could help you," said the snail kindly, "But I carry my house with me and it is only big enough for one."

And as the snail tucked itself snugly inside its home, it realized that there were some good points to being a snail.

# The Snow Queen

**L**ong ago, a wicked sprite made a magic mirror. In it, anything that was good and beautiful had an evil, ugly reflection. One day the mirror was dropped and it smashed into a billion pieces. The wind picked up the fragments and carried them all over the world.

One day a little boy called Kay was playing with his friend, Gerda, when suddenly he cried, "Oh, I've got something in my eye!" It was one of the pieces from the magic mirror! Very quickly, Kay became cruel. He no longer wanted to play with Gerda, and teased her.

One day soon after, Kay saw a large, horse-drawn sleigh glide into the town square. The driver was a woman wrapped in a white fur cloak. Kay did not know it, but she was the wicked Snow Queen.

"Come and warm up in my sleigh," she coaxed. Kay climbed in and the Snow Queen kissed his forehead – and with that kiss Kay forgot his home, his family and Gerda.

The Snow Queen cracked the whip and they soon reached her palace. There Kay stayed with the Snow Queen, having forgotten everything he had once known.

Back home, Gerda decided to look for Kay. After walking for miles she met some wood pigeons who told her, "We've seen Kay! He was sitting in the Snow Queen's sleigh. Ask the reindeer to show you the way."

The reindeer agreed to take Gerda, and they rode through snowy forests and over icy mountains, until they arrived in Lapland. The reindeer took Gerda right up to the Snow Queen's glittering ice palace.

"Her sleigh is gone — the Snow Queen is away," said the reindeer.

Gerda went inside and found herself in an empty, icy, endless hall. And there sat Kay. Gerda ran to him joyfully, but he just sat there, making patterns in the ice.

"Kay!" Gerda whispered. "Don't you remember me?" Kay just sat, numb and motionless.

Then Gerda began to cry. Her warm tears fell on Kay and melted away the Snow Queen's icy kiss. He slowly began to remember his friend and he burst into tears too.

"Gerda! Where am I? Why is it so cold?" Kay wept so much that the splinter of mirror in his eye was washed out.

"The Snow Queen took you," Gerda explained. "Now come with me — we must escape."

Hand in hand the two ran out of the vast hall and climbed onto the friendly reindeer's back. He flew them through the snowy night, until at last they reached the warmth of their homes.

DECEMBER
29

# The Fox and the Snail

One day a fox challenged a snail to a race. "You're on!" said the snail.

The snail set off — very slowly. The fox decided that he had time to stop for a nap. While he slept, the snail climbed onto the fox's tail.

When the fox woke up the snail was nowhere to be seen. He started running, and just before he crossed the finish line he stopped. He still couldn't see the snail. So he called out, "Snail, are you coming soon?"

"I'm already here!" answered the snail — for he had taken this chance to climb down the fox's tail and creep over the finish line.

# The Prophet Elijah
# Visits Earth

The Prophet Elijah and a companion were travelling and needed a place to stay for the night. They came to the cottage of a poor couple and asked if they could stay with them. The couple treated them kindly, feeding them the last of their food. That night, the couple's cow sadly died.

The next night, the Prophet went to ask for shelter at a rich man's house. The man lodged them in his stable and gave them only scraps to eat.

The next day the Prophet repaired the rich man's wall. His companion did not understand. "Why did the poor man lose his cow when he treated you well, and the rich man get rewarded for treating you badly?"

The Prophet answered, "The poor man's wife would have died that night, but I asked God to take the cow instead. The rich man would have found a heap of gold hidden in the wall if I hadn't repaired it."

# The Wild Boar and the Fox

**O**ne fine day, a fox was wandering through a forest, minding his own business, when he came across a wild boar. The boar was hard at work rubbing his white tusks against the bark of a tree to make them sharp.

The fox looked all around. Then he sniffed the air. He could neither see nor smell any hunters that the boar might need to fight off — nor indeed any other dangers.

"My friend, why are you doing that?" asked the fox. "I cannot think of a reason why you are so hard at work preparing your tusks for battle."

"True, comrade," replied the boar. "But the instant my life is in danger I shall need my tusks. There'll be no time to sharpen them then. I like to be prepared."

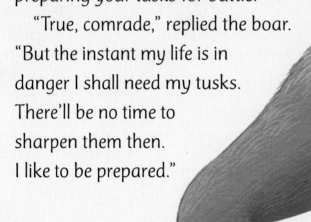

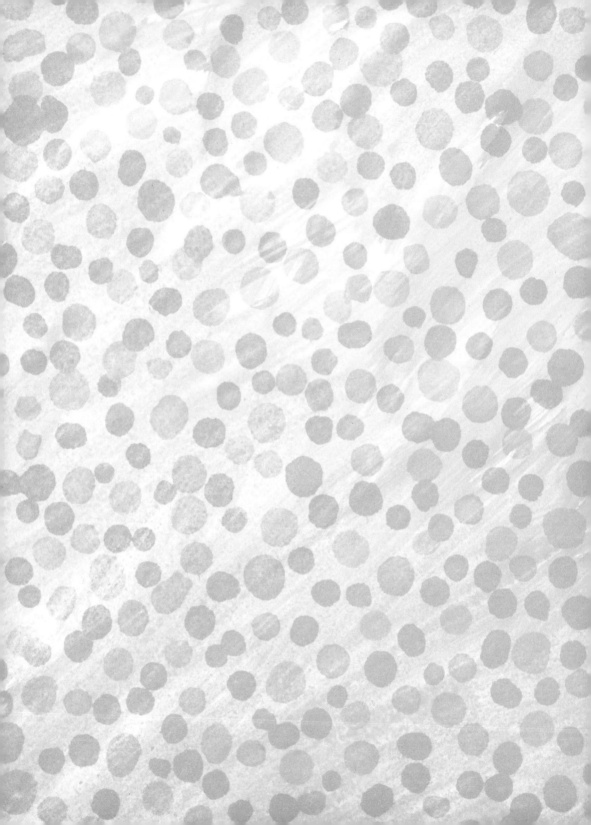